Praise for Ellen Lesser's

THE SHOPLIFTER'S APPRENTICE

"These eleven supple stories quietly, deftly probe the complicated relations of their characters. . . . *The Shoplifter's Apprentice,* outstanding for its lyricism and control, is a pleasure to read."

—*Publishers Weekly*

"Lesser's great strength as a writer is her willingness to undo stereotypical situations and to explore them with zest and compassion. *The Shoplifter's Apprentice* is a delight."

—*Yale*

"Best of all is the title story, a spooky parable . . . a dazzling allegory that entices like Pandora's box."

—*The New York Times Book Review*

AND
The Other Woman

"Each character will make your blood boil; each will melt your poor, unsuspecting heart."

—Sharon Sheehe Stark,
author of *A Wrestling Season*

"Realistic and satisfying. . . .True-to-life characters, guaranteed to spark recognition and emotions."

—Jill McCorkle,
author of *The Cheer Leader*

"There is not one line in this book, not one *phrase,* that isn't true to human nature."

—Carolyn Chute,
author of *The Beans of Egypt, Maine*

Books by Ellen Lesser

The Other Woman
The Shoplifter's Apprentice

Published by WASHINGTON SQUARE PRESS

Most Washington Square Press Books are available at special quantity discounts for bulk purchases for sales promotions, premiums or fund raising. Special books or book excerpts can also be created to fit specific needs.

For details write the office of the Vice President of Special Markets, Pocket Books, 1230 Avenue of the Americas, New York, New York 10020.

THE SHOPLIFTER'S APPRENTICE

STORIES

BY

ELLEN LESSER

WASHINGTON SQUARE PRESS
PUBLISHED BY POCKET BOOKS

New York   London   Toronto   Sydney   Tokyo   Singapore

These stories first appeared, in somewhat different form, in the following magazines:

"The Shoplifter's Apprentice" and "Eating Air" in *The Missouri Review;* "Sara's Friend" and "Stinking Benjamin" in *Indiana Review;* "For Solo Piano" and "Pearlcorder" in *The Louisville Review;* "Dream Life" in *Epoch;* "Pressure for Pressure" in *Green Mountains Review;* "Life Drawing" in *Mississippi Review;* and "Madame Bartova's School of Ballet" in *The Chariton Review.* "Passover Wine" was a winner in the National Invitational Competition for Emerging Writers, sponsored by the NEA and *Passages North,* and appeared in that magazine.

The author gratefully acknowledges permission to use lyrics from the song "ABC," written by The Corporation and published by Jobete Music Co., Inc., © 1970.

A Washington Square Press Publication of
POCKET BOOKS, a division of Simon & Schuster Inc.
1230 Avenue of the Americas, New York, NY 10020

Lesser, Ellen.
  The shoplifter's apprentice stories / Ellen Lesser.
    p.   cm.
  Contents: The shoplifter's apprentice—Sara's friend—
Pearlcorder—Stinking Benjamin—For solo piano—Eating air—
Passover wine—Dream life—Pressure for pressure—Life drawing
—Madame Bartova's School of Ballet.
  Reprint. Originally published in New York : Simon and
Schuster.
  ISBN 0-671-69318-2
  I. Title.
PS3562.E836S56   1990
813'.54—dc20   90-11987
                                                    CIP

First Washington Square Press printing July 1990

10 9 8 7 6 5 4 3 2 1

FOR MY MOTHER AND FATHER

Acknowledgments

I would like to thank Sena Jeter Naslund, Gladys Swan, Gordon Weaver and Sharon Sheehe Stark, for their contributions to the growth of these stories; Debbie Sontag and Mary La Chapelle, for their support and suggestions; John Pickering, for liking this book enough to make something happen; and most of all Roger Weingarten, for living with the stories almost as closely as I did, through all of their incarnations.

Contents

The Shoplifter's Apprentice

She rounded the corner into the aisle that had the beer and chilled wine and almost crashed into a man holding open the flap of his parka, stuffing an inside pocket with what looked like a bottle of champagne. He was so thin and the jacket so big that when he jerked it across his chest, the bottle was swallowed up—except for a barely discernible curve of glass against nylon, invisible.

The man had purplish rings beneath dark eyes that filmed over with what must have been fear for an instant. But then the twin arcs of his heavy eyebrows imposingly merged. His eyes took on a commanding expression. She forgot about getting a bottle of wine. She fled the aisle with a terrible chemical rush in her limbs, as if she were the one who'd been caught in the act of some wrongdoing.

From the checkout line she scanned the aisles of the store, but the man was nowhere in sight. She had to forget him. This had nothing to do with her. She'd never stolen a thing in her life, or just about never. She had tried to take a pack of gum once when she was seven. She hadn't been able to look at the storekeeper's face when he'd asked her the question, only out the window at her waiting bicycle.

When she left the market, the man was waiting for her on the sidewalk.

"Don't worry. I didn't turn you in," she said. "I'm not going to turn you in."

He said, "I know. I hope you'll let me thank you for that." He smiled and glanced suggestively down at the bulge in his coat.

Beneath the oversized parka he was dressed neatly: Levi's, stiff and dark blue; sky blue running sneakers with hardly a scuff mark; a wine-colored turtleneck. Strands of silver laced his black hair, but she wouldn't have put him much over thirty. She had to admit he was strangely handsome, with his skin so pale it was almost diaphanous, and his eyes set deep inside those dark rings. His whole person seemed to have an edge to it. He didn't just stand there on the street, he vibrated.

"You were going to buy some wine, weren't you? But then you didn't."

She wanted to say, "How do you know?" But she hated to give him the advantage. She said, "Not necessarily."

"Listen, don't be like that. I'm a respectable guy. You can have me checked out. I teach at the day-care center on Juniper."

"What do you teach the kids to do?" She was proud of herself now. "Steal from the candy store?"

He grabbed her arm and said, "Are you crazy?" He pulled her into the doorway next to the store and fixed her again with those eyes from the wine aisle. "I don't need this crap from you."

"I'm sorry," she said, wondering at how things had gotten twisted around.

"I live a few blocks away," he said. "You want to come up and drink this champagne, or not?"

He put on an impatient, indifferent face, but she could feel the pressure of his grip through her coat sleeve.

The man's apartment, on the third floor of a yellow Victorian, resembled more than anything a warehouse, or a flea market. Hung from nails along the entryway wall was a wardrobe of cowboy hats with ornate, feathered hatbands, Greek fisherman's caps, felt fedoras. Rising from the far corner of the living-room floor like some unearthly shrubbery was a collection of fire extinguishers. Bordering that were stacks of brand-new hardcover books and a tower of cassette tapes, still in cellophane. A long, low table was crowded with digital clock-radios, Chinese porcelain, paperweights, empty picture frames. His one window was draped with a dozen glass crystals that quivered in the still air, disturbing the walls with prism colors. There was nothing casual about this man's shoplifting.

He came in from the kitchen with tall champagne glasses, cut-glass flutes with gold lips. The champagne was Dom Perignon. He'd left on the price tag: fifty-seven fifty. He motioned her toward a couch covered in a patchwork of woven Indian rugs and tilted the glasses to the stream of champagne. He touched his glass to hers and held it there. He looked at her until she had to turn away.

She made a circle around the room with her glass. "I don't believe all this. What do you do it for?"

"Got to have some excitement in this town." His half-smile was impudent, almost a dare, a suggestion that perhaps she, too, needed some.

"What happens when you get caught?"

"I don't." He emptied his champagne in one long draft. "It's that simple."

"How can you say that? *I* caught you, didn't I?"

"That's different."

"Why? I could have reported you."

"But you didn't."

He smiled an inscrutable smile. He filled his glass again and seemed to forget her for a moment, staring into the effervescing pale gold. The late-winter sky darkened behind the curtain of crystals, and dusk began to gather like fog around the things in the room. In the silence she thought she could feel him and all his strange loot vibrating at the same frequency. When it was almost dark, he stepped quietly around and lit candles—low, fat ones and long, slender tapers in candlesticks. A motley forest of shadows rose up. The light played tricks with the bony planes of his face. She wished it not to be so, but she wanted him.

When she woke the next morning, he was already gone. For a second she didn't know where she was. Then she recognized the striped flannel sheets, the hand-loomed wool blanket. He'd left a pot of coffee on the stove. In the refrigerator were a bag of croissants, a drawer full of cheese—Emmenthaler, Montrachet, Gorgonzola, smoked Gouda—and door racks lined with fancy jellies and jams. She stood at the counter and nibbled on a croissant spread with sweet butter and Swedish lingonberry preserves, she sipped the strong coffee. She was pleased she had slept with him. She remembered her head and shoulders and chest hanging over the edge of the bed and feeling like she was falling.

She picked up her clothes from where they lay in a heap on the bedroom floor. Next to the bed was an old black camp trunk, covered with carved wooden boxes. The first one she opened was empty. She tried one more, then another. She set the boxes on the bed and opened the trunk. It was full of clothes—not his, for a woman: a silk blouse, midnight blue; a baby pink feather boa; a pair of black satin jeans; a big, soft leather pouch of a shoulder bag.

The jeans were a skimpy size six. She held the blouse up to her. It would be too small across the chest, in the shoulders. She sifted through the trunk, and from successive layers came glimpses of turquoise and peach, of lace and angora. There was a woman he'd stolen it for, slender and stylish, a woman who was nothing like her. Either the woman had left all the clothes behind when she'd left him, or he hadn't found her yet.

* * *

Fingering garments she could never hope to buy on store racks, daydreaming over pictures in magazines, eating spaghetti and rice while she saved for the season's one extravagant purchase—she was as much prey to disproportionate material longings as anyone. But after the night at the shoplifter's, what had been idle desires took on a tangible urgency. When she picked up her bar of Ivory, she imagined a shelf full of luxury soaps—honey-almond, green apple, lime oil, wild lavender—so real she could practically smell them. Staring into the rack of lifeless clothes in her closet, she thought of the trunk, like a Pandora's Box. Almadén Mountain Chablis, long her staple, had a sour new bite on her tongue. Having to wait for books to come out in paperback suddenly seemed an injustice. And she thought about him, the way his eyes in their purple shadows had shone in the dark, the way he had taken her clothes off and touched her as if she belonged to him.

"I was in the neighborhood," she told him when he opened the door. He didn't seem surprised to see her. She found a place on the couch, between a pile of plastic-wrapped pink and yellow Oxford cloth shirts and a twenty-five-foot extension cord.

"I gather you found your way around the other morning?" he called from the kitchen, and from his tone she imagined a sneer on his face. She wondered if he knew she had opened the trunk. He came back with glasses and a liter of Alsatian beer. "So you don't find me vile and reprehensible?"

She said, "No. I like you," but the words felt like paste in her mouth. It was hard to imagine, seeing him now, that they'd ever made love. Out the window the day was overcast, and in the dull light he looked gaunt, unnatural. There was something sad or dead about so much merchandise lying about the apartment unused, something criminal in the waste of it.

"Oh, I don't know." He smiled out of one side of his

mouth. "Let's say you're intrigued by me." He eyed her, sipping his beer. "By my habit."

She started to protest, but instead tilted her head in a wordless assent.

"You working tomorrow?"

"Not until the dinner shift. Why?"

"Want to come around with me?"

"Come around?"

"Yeah. Saturday's a good day. You need anything?"

The shoplifter's primer: Step one, know your store. Act premeditatively, not on impulse. Check for tv cameras, electronic eyes, convex mirrors hanging in corners. Distinguish shop employees from customers. Study their work patterns. Is the establishment understaffed? Or are there extra clerks with time on their hands, loafing, keeping an eye out? What are the lines of sight from the register desk and other clerk outposts? Where are the blind spots, the safety zones?—almost every store has them. And don't forget mirrors. Your own reflection could be your undoing.

He explained all this over breakfast and as they drove the few blocks from his place to the downtown shops in his '68 Rambler wagon. A spring poked through the seat and into her thigh. They could have walked, but he needed the car to deposit things. She hadn't slept very well. His lovemaking this time had been perfunctory, tired. Afterward, she must have lain awake a long while listening to his nasal breath, to a constellation of small, unfamiliar noises.

"The main thing is to follow your instincts," he was saying, driving slowly around the municipal lot. "Sometimes everything looks just right, but you get this funny feeling." He put a hand to his stomach. "Other times you can pull off just about anything."

He eased the car between a van and a pickup truck. "You

happen to notice the hats as you come into my place? Know how I got most of those? Ready for this? I put them on my head and just walked out of the store."

"No. Come on. You walked out with a hat on your head and nobody noticed?"

Their first stop was a clothing store named Avocado. March was bitter and blustery, but on the racks of Avocado a gentler season had already installed itself, a warm wind on her body through billowing cotton clothes. He whispered into her ear, "Make like you're looking around," and headed for the back of the store, toward the men's section and "Winter Clearance" sign. There were two saleswomen up at the desk, one middle-aged and one young. The older one said something quietly to the other, and they both looked toward the back. Then the younger woman was coming out from behind the desk, walking toward her. An alarm went off in every cell in her body.

When the saleswoman met her eyes, she smiled a smile that felt sick at the sides of her mouth. She couldn't tell if the other woman was smiling back normally.

The saleswoman stopped halfway to the back at a shelf of summer sweaters, and began to refold them. Maybe that was it. Maybe nothing was going to happen. Her blood slowed a little and a sour ache settled into her arms and legs.

She didn't turn around, but she could feel the woman at the front watching her. She approached a rack of lacy Victorian blouses and stopped to study each one in turn, tilting her head to the side, fashioning a face of serious consideration. She held up one shirt and stared at it. Her heart leaped when she felt his hand on her arm.

"Let's go," he said under his breath.

She said, "What?" just as his words came clear to her.

"Just walk straight out. Stay in front of me."

She put the blouse back and turned to the door. She didn't

know her legs when she went to walk on them. As she moved she could feel the saleswoman's eyes from behind and also him, following close, like an ill-fitting shadow.

Only at the end of the block did she dare to look at him, at the tremendous swelling inside his jacket. No one had followed them out. No one was coming after them. The ache she'd felt all the way from the store turned into a strange, high hum of the blood. A crazy giggle broke out of her. "Let's get to the car," he said. "Fast." She half-ran to keep up with him.

In the driver's seat, he caught his breath. He thrust a hand up under his jacket and pulled out a bundle of thick, gray, heathery wool—a fisherman's sweater. He looked around through the windows, then held it up to his chest for a moment. "Should fit," he said. "Think it looks good on me?"

She nodded and tried to look cheerful, telling herself that next time he'd get something for her. He folded the sweater and slipped it under an old blanket he kept across the back seat, looked around again and popped his door open.

In Capitol Books, she browsed through the new hardcover novels. He came up to her and said, "Ready to go?" He led her out, pressing into her side. She could feel the hard edges of books through his jacket. For himself, he'd gotten an oversized, illustrated *Great Wines of France*. For her, *The Bedside Compendium of Crime*. Detective stories weren't her favorite.

In the Blues Connection, he shoved a pair of woman's designer jeans under his jacket. Not half a minute later, the salesman at the desk, who looked like the manager or even the owner, picked up the telephone. The man dialed, waited for a moment, hung up. She looked for the bulge in the shoplifter's jacket and then at his face, for some sign that it didn't worry him.

"Let's hope they're your size," he said on the way back to the car.

"Thirty?"

"I'm not sure."

The jeans were stone-washed denim with little pleats at the hips, size twenty-seven. "These might have fit me when I was fifteen," she said.

He shrugged. "How am I supposed to know what size you wear? You could help me out, you know."

There were no other shoppers in the Craft Gallery. The sales desk too was empty for a moment, and then a saleswoman appeared from behind a curtain and said, "Good morning." She smiled back and lingered by the shelves of ceramic mugs, oil lamps and honey pots, holding one up to the window to admire the glaze, testing another for weight. The saleswoman said, "Let me know if I can be of any help" and disappeared again.

He was standing in a corner along the back wall. He motioned her over. He was holding a hand-knitted sweater, light blue flecked with gray, lambswool or mohair. The tag was inside the collar: Medium. She nodded. "Stand right there," he said. "Don't move." She was close enough to feel his quickened pulse as he worked the sweater under his jacket, and she imagined for an instant that he was aroused. The saleswoman came back out just as he was finishing.

In Champion Sporting Goods she lost track of him and found herself in a corner by a rack of sunglasses. She looked out at the store from between the rack's plastic tiers. She couldn't see any salespeople. In a matter of a few seconds she could take down a pair of glasses, fold it, slip it into her coat pocket. That navy blue mirrored pair. She could almost feel it pulling on her, drawing her in, like an undertow. Yet the finest of veils seemed to hang between her and the rack, and to draw that veil aside, to move her hand—it made her weak to think of it.

At the end of the afternoon, they sat in the car. She looked from him to the back seat, where the blanket covered the uneven terrain of his acquisitions.

"You have to go now, right?" he said.

He took a brown paper A & P bag from under the car seat and held it open.

She'd pushed the bag under her own car seat and driven to the restaurant, where she was just a couple of minutes late for her shift. She changed into her uniform and started wiping down the silverware for her station without saying much to anyone. Most of what was in the bag was of no use to her, but the sweater was beautiful. While her first party finished their cocktails, she thought about how cold he'd been when he dropped her off at her car. He hadn't said a word about getting together.

She went through the shift absentmindedly, bringing the hors d'oeuvres to the wrong table, forgetting a second bottle of Sauvignon Blanc. While she cleared plates and set fresh places she thought of the feeling she'd had at the last couple of stores, like the benign, even pleasurable panic she got at the movies, worrying but deep down knowing the hero would prevail. Or she stood, in her mind, in front of the sunglass rack, pushing against whatever it was that had held her hand back—some failure of imagination, the inertia of honesty. She tried to picture her hand, weightless, like it wasn't her hand, reaching up to the glasses.

When she'd punched out and picked up a moderate evening's tips, she noticed him standing in the restaurant entryway. She wished she'd already changed out of her uniform.

"I've got a present for you," he said. His hands were behind his back, hiding it.

"Right here?" She looked to see that no one was watching them.

"Do you want it or not?"

He brought it out in front of him, a bundle made of a shopping bag that had seen some wear. She didn't know why she'd expected something wrapped, or at least in a box. Of course he wouldn't be giving her that kind of present. Inside the shopping bag was a supple mass of brown leather. She realized she'd seen it before, in the clothes trunk. Now she felt it, the finest and smoothest of skins. The purse was enormous, amorphous, enveloping. Whatever she put inside would get lost somewhere deep in the folds.

"If you like it, it's yours." One side of his mouth pulled into a smirk. In the dimmed light of the restaurant foyer his eyes looked almost sardonic. "I thought you might be able to make good use of it."

That night she dreamed of trooping after the shoplifter from store to store, the way after a day at the ocean she would feel over and over the undertow drawing her down and back, the breaking waves washing her forward. Now and then she'd shake herself out of sleep, as if to come up for air, and she'd see the leather bag on the night table, slumped over the edge like a sleeping animal.

Sunday morning she got up to make tea and then went back to bed. She thought on and off about the shoplifter and his gift as she lay there and dozed. Even when she was fully awake, she stayed in bed for a long time thinking—but no longer of him. She was remembering something she'd read years before about dreams, controlling them. Before you went to sleep, you were supposed to think very hard about a particular physical movement, like taking a step. Then, in your dream, you were to perform the movement, willfully, against the dream's momentum, against a resistance like heavy water. When you willed your leg to take that step, you would feel a dimension of power, a tangible physicality, such as you'd never before in a dream experienced. She thought about how it would be that same kind of feeling to stand in front of the sunglass rack and move her hand.

Monday, she packed everything she'd need for the day into the leather bag—a lunch, her makeup case, her uniform, the black Chinese shoes she wore for waitressing.

She was the first customer at Avocado that morning. There was only one saleswoman, who hadn't been there on Saturday, up at the register, reading a paper. She wandered among the racks, glancing back at the saleswoman, watching herself come and go in the shop mirrors.

It was just a small thing—a pair of crazy striped tights in a little plastic pouch. She didn't know if it was the right size. She checked in the mirrors, as if not to be reflected was to be invisible. Her hand felt very much like her hand when she took it, then shoved it down deep under all the other things in the bag. What felt different was the rest of her. This rush of chemicals wasn't only fear, it was a terrible freedom. Anything could happen now.

Sara's Friend

When I took the East Fifth Street apartment, no one said anything about a group home on the block—not the agent, not the super, not the woman who had the apartment before. But the day I moved in I saw two of the people.

I needed some coffee, and wasn't ready to face the two-burner hot plate advertised as a kitchenette, so I walked down toward the Binibon Cafe, at the corner of Second Avenue. Before I went in, I looked back up the block. The brownstones weren't elegant, or even especially well kept, but they were better than the tenements where I'd found sublets—two months here, three there—in the year since I'd left home. A line of skinny trees rose from the sidewalk, pitiful but miraculous, their few leaves like tattered paper in the afternoon breeze. A couple of figures caught my eye, clambering down the steps of a brownstone, stopping to listen to a woman who spoke from the doorway. At first I thought they were teenagers, but when I looked again I could see they were men.

The first one down wore overalls and a T-shirt and carried a plastic bat and ball. He made an exaggerated show of looking both ways, then positioned himself in the middle of the street. He tossed the ball up and caught it a few times before swinging and hitting it. Then he let out a shout and ran in my direction, yelling something like "Banzai!" or "Bull's-eye!" The ball rolled under a car and into the gutter. In a minute he emerged from behind a Volkswagen, laughing, holding his dripping trophy high in the air.

The other man had a crew cut and wore his shirt buttoned all the way to the neck. He also worked his way toward the Binibon end of the block, but quietly, stopping by each car and peering inside with a flicker of something like memory passing over his face, as if he'd parked there some time ago and forgotten which car belonged to him.

I didn't want them to notice me, so I turned the corner and ducked into the Binibon. There was a perfectly ordinary man at the counter reading a newspaper. The Binibon served refills for ten cents, and I drank until my insides turned shaky. When I finally left, the block was empty again, and the house the two men had come from was shut up tight, indistinguishable from the others except for the window grates that went up all four stories.

I bought a mattress and a small desk and chair—delivery included—from a furniture warehouse. I set the desk up on the window wall, for the light, and also to have some distraction while I was proofreading. The street was quiet for most of the day, but like clockwork, at five minutes past three, the people from the group home came down the block from the Bowery side, back from one of those schools or special factories where they counted a certain number of envelopes into a plastic bag, or sorted nuts from bolts, or filled little cardboard boxes with paper clips—some necessary but marginal task, like me sitting there scanning the galley proofs of technical magazines for misspellings, seeing the sentences and paragraphs and articles only as accretions of individual words, giving no thought to how they fit together into some larger pattern, how they might mean something.

The baseball player I'd seen my first day was always the most energetic, running up and down the line, hopping back

and forth, laughing and teasing somebody. There was a black
girl with a tinny transistor radio. She didn't walk but danced up
the sidewalk, the notes breaking and jumping as she dipped
and turned. Sometimes the baseball player tried to cut in and
dance with her. She gave him a slap or shooed him off, and
then he went for the radio. She hugged the transistor to her
bony chest and sprinted up the street, yelling, "Carmen!" or
"Larry!" He laughed and pretended to hug something to the
bib of his overalls.

The others cowered a little, shrank up inside themselves, as
they followed: the older man with the crew cut, who always
looked just short of some great discovery; another black girl,
whose face I never saw full on, but who had something wrong
with her nose, as though it were split down the middle into
two noses; a chubby white boy with a face like a full moon
and a perpetual smile, stupid or unfathomably good; and always last in line, a woman with black therapeutic shoes who
pushed her feet forward, one at a time, as if the shoes had
lead weights in them. Moving down the street seemed to take
all her concentration. But now and then, for no apparent reason outside of herself, she broke for just a moment into a
kind of grimace I read as a smile. I wondered what small triumph from her day at school, what bright shard of childhood
memory, had jostled her amid that grim progress.

The home was across the street and a few doors down from
my building, so I could watch them all walk past and up the
steps. I couldn't see much of anything inside when the door
opened, just a glimpse of a young woman with curly black
hair—maybe Carmen—who ushered them in. Then they were
swallowed up, the block reasserted its shabby decorum, and I
always felt a little emptier looking down at the dizzying gray
of words on my proofreader's galley, behind me at my three
walls. I tried to finish up the stack of articles I had set for that
day—the sooner I returned them, the sooner I got paid—but I
found my eyes drifting back to that inscrutably ordinary fa-

cade, wondering what it was like in there, if they had their own rooms, if the baseball player got punished for his attempts on the radio.

The Binibon was always quiet, so quiet I didn't know how it stayed in business. There were never more than three or four customers, and though there was a menu and a small kitchen out back, I never saw anyone order food. I always took one particular window table, under an enormous Wandering Jew. I brought magazines, half-finished letters home, sometimes even my proofreading. I sat with my back to the length of my block and looked out toward the Avenue, where the cars sped by like ghost ships behind the steamed glass. Whenever the brass bell sounded and the heavy glass door was pushed open, I paid attention, as if some new piece of my life were about to walk in. The last person I expected to see that late afternoon was the woman from the home—the one with the therapeutic shoes.

She was wearing a pant suit, spruce green polyester. Her face looked mannish, with its square jaw and the shadow of hair over her upper lip. Once the door creaked shut behind her, she turned her head from right to left, as if her eyes couldn't move independently. When she caught sight of me she smiled, and it was like a little light turning on somewhere inside, how it softened her. She stepped deliberately toward my side of the cafe. For a minute I thought she was coming right to my table. Instead, she sat at the next one, facing me. When she'd maneuvered her bottom down onto the chair, she wet her lips. She said, "Hey," very loud, as if she were calling from across the whole restaurant.

I met her eyes for a second, then dived into my magazine.

The waitress took a long time coming out from the back. The woman from the home said, "Please. Coffee, thank you," also very loud and careful, nervous but triumphant, as though they were foreign words she'd learned from a phrasebook and practiced over and over before she came in. She took a few coins out of her jacket pocket and held them out, her palm bright with sweat.

The waitress said, "Hold it for now, honey," and the woman looked confused. She drew her head down into her chest and her smile turned in on itself. I peeked up at her again when the coffee came. She filled the cup to the brim with cream and then proceeded to empty in three whole packets of Sweet 'n Low.

"Lady."

I hoped she was calling the waitress, but she was looking at me.

"You some pretty lady. Yeah," she said, nodding her head up and down. "You real pretty." She ran her two hands down the sides of her face toward her breasts and cocked her head sideways, coquettish but lurid at the same time, like a homely kid imitating a movie star. I couldn't help laughing. She winced and tucked her head in, even further than she had with the waitress. She stared with big, sad cow eyes into her cup, the saucer a pool of almost white coffee. I thought she might even cry. I had to do something.

"I'm sorry," I said. "I wasn't laughing at you."

She looked across at me, still suspicious. "Carmen says it's good to be nice with the people." Her speech was thick, as if her tongue were too fat for her mouth. "Carmen says Sara go for coffee if Sara be good."

"You are good," I said. "You're very nice."

"Yeah?" She smiled again, but tentatively. "You be nice with Sara?"

"Sure," I said. "Sure." I looked around, but the waitress had disappeared again. I slid a dollar bill under the edge of my cup. "Listen, I've got to go."

She arranged herself in the seat and smoothed down the

lines of her jacket. She looked calm now, back to herself. I waited a minute to see if she would say anything else. She gave me a dignified nod, as if she were dismissing me, and looked suddenly older, worn out. "Sara have coffee now."

I stayed away from the Binibon for a couple of weeks after that. When I went back, there were a few more customers than I'd been used to, probably because of the early November chill, but my old table was free. I ordered coffee and splurged on a piece of carrot cake. Through the window I could see the last in Fifth Street's line of sidewalk trees, already looking half dead, leaves dried up but still clinging. I was staring out at it, warming my hands on my cup, when all of a sudden there was the woman, standing over me, smiling. "Remember Sara?"

She kept smiling and standing there, her breath sour-smelling and labored, until I realized she wasn't going to leave. She said, "Sara sit down?" and her face twisted up, half excited, half as if she were expecting a blow.

"Sure. Okay. I mean, I'm going in a few minutes, but . . ."

Sara sat, and placed one moist palm over my hand, which I hadn't realized was gripping the side of the table. "You stay now," she said. "You be nice with Sara."

When the waitress came I managed to pull my hand back and hide it in my lap. Sara and the waitress seemed friendly now. The woman asked, "What would you like today?" even though Sara must have ordered the same thing every time, with the same studied good manners. She put her two quarters down by the sugar caddy before her cup came, lined them up neatly and touched each one again. "Pretty lady stay with Sara," she said when the waitress brought coffee. I must have turned to the woman helpless, disavowing, full of an unbecoming irony. She shot me back a harsh look. I smiled weakly at Sara and ordered a refill.

Sara went through her routine with the Sweet 'n Low and

cream, then bent to the cup and drank off an inch or so. "This your neighborhood?"

"Not exactly."

She considered this, then nodded as if I had told her something important. Just then the door flew open in an angry chiming of bells. It was the black girl from the home, the one with the radio. She spun around until she spotted Sara and marched up to the table with long, sure, angular strides. "Carmen say you got to come now," she panted. She turned to me and patted my arm, as if to console me. "Sara got to go now."

Sara stood up slowly, checked her pockets, checked the table for her coins. The black girl danced around her. "Carmen be mad you don't hurry." She tugged on Sara's arm. Sara could hardly walk between struggling into her ski jacket and trying to look back at me. From the door she raised her arm halfheartedly. I turned to watch the black girl drag her across the street and up the block, out of sight. Then I was startled by a different image, murky through the steam and grime on the glass: my own face and behind it, the punk wallpaper of broadsides over the boarded-up newsstand.

Since night had started falling so soon, I took to waking up earlier. Shortly before eight o'clock, the people from the home left for school—not as lively as on the way back, a little like somnambulists buttoned up against the chill morning. Sara had a new ski jacket, bright baby blue. Sometimes she walked next to the older man with the crew cut, silently, shoulder to shoulder, with the air of a couple married forever, an air not exactly of happiness but of deep peace. Sometimes the baseball player and the radio girl even walked together like a brother and sister observing a truce from their usual bickering. Once the people were gone, I went out myself. I liked being on the street at that hour when everyone was hurrying off to work. The city had a thousand corner coffee shops, hundreds of little cafes, with the same trays of croissants, the same tins

of oversized bran muffins. I could go to any one of them, order
my coffee, pretend I was an acting student, a writer, pretend
I lived in the neighborhood.

In the hours between ten and three I did most of my proofreading. I was getting faster, and since I'd been with the company almost a year, they were giving me better assignments—
fewer of the technical magazines, more from the young-adult
book division. Sometimes I'd find myself not just scanning the
lines for mistakes, but reading, getting caught up in the stories. I actually read one through from beginning to end—about
a teenage girl with a mildly retarded sister.

Marion always says she's an only child and never brings
friends home after school. When it comes time for her Sweet
Sixteen, she has to decide: either give up the party or let out
her secret. She has a crush on a boy in her English class, Peter,
and inviting him to a Sweet Sixteen is one way to get him to
notice her. Marion's mother buys the sister a new dress for the
party, and unlike the sixteen-year-old, who's still in a training
bra, the sister is *developing*. On the first slow number Peter
asks her to dance.

Only later, when he asks Marion where her "friend" comes
from, does he find out the truth. Marion tells him, then runs
up to her bedroom. Her mother knocks quietly and pushes the
door open, sits down on the bed, dabs at Marion's bleeding
mascara and says things like *She's a young woman too.* When
Marion finally goes back down to the party, she finds her sister
surrounded by a group of the girls, talking and smiling. "Hey,
Marion," one calls out. "How come you've been keeping your
sister all to yourself?" As Marion gropes for an answer, she
feels a hand on her shoulder. Of course it's Peter, who's liked
her all along, who really wanted to dance with her in the first
place.

The Best Birthday Present. That's what it was called. I
could just picture the cover: Marion with her tears, her dark
brow. Over one shoulder, a smaller Peter, with wavy brown

hair and full mouth. And on the other side, the sister, in her yellow chiffon and her breasts, looking unreal and perfect—somebody's idea of the lovable victim, the innocent.

My concentration was always broken when the people from the group home came back. I'd shower and dress, even put on a skirt sometimes—not for that mythical someone I might run into, but for myself, to feel solid, professional, as if I might have spent the day somewhere besides my own room. Then I'd go down to the Binibon. Sara's privilege of afternoon coffee had become a regular part of her schedule. She came in at four-fifteen, and with a confidence that grew from repetition, she stood by the door, surveying the tables. Sometimes she just called a loud, proprietary hello to me and then made her plodding way to the counter, where, with some difficulty, she set herself up on a stool. I wondered if someone from the home hadn't told her to sit by herself, not to bother the other customers, because those days she seemed to have a stoical self-satisfaction about her. Sometimes I caught her reflection in the mirror facing the counter, eyeing me sheepishly, with regret. I no longer minded when she did sit down with me. I was curious about the group home, and though trying to hold a conversation was painstaking, I'd started to piece together a picture.

Some days she was fixated on one thing, like the fact that she'd slipped in the bathroom and gotten a black-and-blue knee, or that Barbara, the radio girl, called her Fatso, or that one day she'd visit her aunt and uncle in Puerto Rico—Carmen had promised her. Whatever I said, she kept replaying the same thing over and over. Those days I was relieved when the waitress came to tell her it was going on five o'clock, and I watched her navigate out of the Binibon and down the block—not really fat: a compact truck of a woman—wondering what it was to have a mind like hers, to be that kind of prisoner.

Other days it was easier. I asked questions, and if I worked to keep her on track, I could learn something. Mornings she had school, where they studied personal hygiene, money, and red and green lights. After lunch she worked in the factory, boxing sets of kids' blocks, making sure each one got all the different colors and shapes. She got paid, according to the number of boxes she packed, every Friday. That was where her coffee money came from. Most of the others saved their money, to buy things in stores, but Sara would rather go to the Binibon. She saved other things, anyway: empty Kleenex boxes, toilet-paper rolls, shampoo bottles. She had them all piled up in her closet. Carmen said one day they were going to have to throw all that junk out. "It's not junk," Sara said, sticking out her fleshy lower lip. "It's Sara's collection."

On weekends, the people got visits from relatives, who took them out places. Some of them even got to stay with their families overnight. Sara didn't have any family, except for that aunt and uncle, and I imagined what it must have been like for her on Saturday mornings, greeting everyone else's relatives in her loud, polite way, watching them, as I sometimes watched from my window, bustling out into the exhilarating air of the regular world. Then she'd go back to her room, take down all her boxes and bottles and rearrange them. In the living room she might find crayons and paper to draw on—trees, flowers and a little house with two stick figures, one with hair turned up at the ends and a triangle skirt. Then she'd get the person on weekend duty to write across the top: *Puerto Rico*.

It was hard to follow her when she got going on this, but there was an organization that sent volunteers to take people like Sara out on the weekends. A couple of times, it had sent a woman for Sara, but Sara hadn't liked her. Something bad had happened when they went out—either Sara got lost or hurt, or she did something to hurt the volunteer—and the woman hadn't come back after that. After Sara told me this she got quiet and stared down into her cup, sneaking glances up at me through her heavy black eyelashes. I didn't let on, but I knew exactly what she was thinking.

In December, I accepted a special proofreading project—a series of pamphlets for junior high and high school health classes: smoking, drinking, drugs, sex, VD, birth control . . . all those kids out there screwing and getting stoned behind their parents' backs, while there I was grown up and free and celibate, my only indulgences a jug of supermarket burgundy, a dollar joint once a week at Washington Square. I stopped going to the Binibon afternoons. To meet the deadline on the pamphlets and also get my other work done meant pushing on well past dark. I decided that when the money came through for the pamphlets, I'd take the rest of what I'd saved and buy a ticket home, surprise the family for Christmas, maybe even have a little left over for presents. The Saturday I finished, I rewarded myself with a few hours' looking in shops—not buying, just scouting.

I was surprised to see Sara come into the Binibon that afternoon, partly because I didn't think she went there on Saturdays, partly because the thoughts of my trip and the shopping had me miles away from that Fifth Street routine. I'd found a rack of big-shouldered, almost ankle-length, fifties tweed coats in a vintage shop. I was picturing myself in one of them, bumping into some good-looking guy on the street, when, out of breath, face beaming, Sara appeared alongside my table. For a minute she was panting too hard to speak, and I had time to take in the way the city soot had begun to dull that astonishing blue of her ski jacket, the way her mittens were clamped like a kid's to the jacket sleeves, the folded piece of red paper in one mittened hand. Even when she seemed to have caught her breath she didn't speak. She set the paper on the table in front of me: a picture of a Christmas tree, done in crayon. Under the tree was not the usual miscellany of packages but a series of black question marks. "Sara draw good?"

"Very good," I said, nodding my head, trying to look really impressed. "And your question marks."

She hunched her shoulders and bobbed her head up and down—Sara's own peculiar manner of laughing—and I laughed too. I realized I'd missed her a little bit. Inside the card was some handwriting clearly not Sara's: *Please join all your friends at the East Village Group Home for a Christmas party, Saturday, December 20, 2 p.m. Bring a small, wrapped gift for the Grab Bag.* At the bottom, she'd written her name in green crayon and drawn a red heart. "Sara don't know lady's name," she said, pointing a mitten at the top of the card where the name would have been written.

I smiled. It was true. In all the times we'd talked, she'd never asked and I'd never come forward. "June," I told her.

She repeated, "June," as if in having been so long withheld the name had acquired some added significance. "June. You come to the party?"

I kept my eyes on the invitation a minute. I had to think fast. The twentieth was the following Saturday. No doubt I'd be running around, getting ready for the trip home, buying my new coat, my presents. And yet I didn't dare look back up at her with *no* on my face. She must have been carrying the invitation back and forth to the Binibon for days—it was ragged around the edges. I closed the card so the Christmas tree faced front again, with its interrogation. I looked up only reluctantly. I could scarcely stand to see her face, that contortion of desire. "Okay," I said, and braced myself for what would come next.

Instead of the wild joy I'd expected, a calm came over her. She straightened her jacket with that purposeful Sara dignity. Then her face went slack, as if she were trying to call back some phrase she'd memorized for the occasion. In the end she shrugged her shoulders, smiled bashfully. "June."

* * *

For all the worries I could have had about the Christmas party, I focused on two: what to wear and what to bring for the Grab Bag. No doubt the people from the home would be in their best clothes, but the only dressy things I had were either low-cut or tight-fitting. And then there was the problem of the present. What could you get for somebody in a group home? What could they use? I thought of a book, but of course they wouldn't read. I saw some nice candles, but what if they started a fire? In the end I found a sale on the next year's calendars and picked one with a different exotic animal for every month. Even if the dates didn't mean much, they could look at the pictures.

During the week before the party, I got all the proofreading done, bought my plane ticket, settled on a half-dozen NEW YORK T-shirts in different colors and sizes. All week a cold wind bit through the wool-lined raincoat my mother had given me as a going-away present when I left Tulsa—a coat that will take you through any weather, she'd told me. I first felt the flu coming on that Saturday in the laundromat. Steamy as it was in there, I got the chills, and over the six blocks to Fifth Street my arms and legs started to ache. By the time I'd dragged the two pillowcases of clothes up to my place, it was noon. I crawled under the blankets still in my raincoat and sneakers and tried to think: I should have skipped the T-shirts and bought that big winter coat. How was I going to drag myself to the airport the next day? And why had I ever agreed to go to the party?

I woke in a sweat, not sure where I was. Then I sat up with a start. But it was only twenty of two. I had just enough time to wash up, dress, wrap the calendar.

When I rang the bell at the home, I was surprised to see a tall, good-looking black man answer the door. I wished I weren't wearing my raincoat, wished that in my haste I'd bothered to put on some makeup. "I'm June."

Before I could get out the rest, he said, "Sara's friend, right? Larry. Good to see you."

I couldn't read his smile—whether it was admiring, or carried a hint of amusement, disdain. I was confused between being ashamed of my connection to Sara, and proud of it.

Just then Sara herself appeared behind him and pulled me in through the doorway. She was wearing a red plaid dress with a ruffle down the front like a schoolgirl's, only the bodice was tight. You could see the white of a slip where the fabric pulled at the buttons. She had a red plastic barrette in her hair and was wearing red lipstick, gaudy on her heavy mouth. "You're here," she said, and then turned to Larry. "June's here."

"Why don't you help June off with her coat?" he said.

Maybe they'd practiced this in preparation for the party. I could see the people lined up in pairs for the drill, taking turns helping each other on and off with their ski jackets. Sara moved toward my raincoat as if she knew exactly what had to be done, but once she'd pulled it partway off, my arms got stuck and we wrestled a minute. From the next room came a Muzak "Joy to the World." When the coat was hung up on a hook, she took hold of my hand. "Now Sara show the people."

The living room stretched the whole length of the brownstone. The walls were covered with fake wood paneling, the floors with brown indoor-outdoor carpeting. An old fold-out buffet table listed against the near wall, bearing trays of Christmas cookies, faded red paper napkins, a punch bowl. The tree sat in the far corner, spindly, anemic, its few branches sagging under the weight of Popsicle-stick and aluminum-foil ornaments. Except for the baseball player, who wore his perennial overalls, starched and clean, all the people from the home were dressed up. They looked uncomfortable in their jumpers and skirts, their hiked-up pants and string ties. They sat stiffly on the matching plaid couches and chairs with plastic cups of punch in their hands, or stood in small groups with what must have been family, barely speaking, trying so hard to be good they'd forgotten it was a party.

The punch had a strange chemical aftertaste, as if Sara had gotten in there with her Sweet 'n Low. I had to alternate between sips and the obligatory cookies: she wouldn't let go of my hand. Then she led me around from group to group, introducing me. My head felt packed tight with cotton and I was starting to get the chills again, so the parade of residents and relatives passed as if at a distance. Sara repeated, "This is June. Sara's friend."

The mothers and fathers shook my free hand and said, "Nice to meet you," as if I played some role in their lives, in their children's lives. The people from the home, whom I felt like I knew, having watched them so many days from my window, either nodded absently or grinned.

For some reason I'd imagined them playing games, like at a kids' party, but this was it: the decorations, the cookies and punch, the stilted imitation of social life and the carols, pumped out metallic and monotonous from some invisible source like a nightmare of Christmas. At the far end of one of the couches a man sat alone, rubbing his hand back and forth in slow motion over his crotch, his eyes placid, elsewhere. No one else paid any attention to his mechanical, dreamy caress, but my eyes kept stealing back, and in spite of myself I felt a little pulse of arousal. Carmen announced that the Grab Bag would take place in fifteen minutes, at three. After that I could make my excuses.

The girl with the double nose came toward the refreshment table and I studied her a minute. If you saw her every day, would hers become just another face like all faces? As I was thinking this, she knocked over a cup of punch, and a few more toppled like dominoes. She looked frightened for a moment, then let out a bellowing laugh that seemed to set off something wild in the others. The radio girl started clapping her hands and singing falsetto: "A-B-C. Easy as one-two-three." Before anyone could stop him, the baseball player had picked up the punch bowl and was prancing around with it, the pink liquid sloshing up over the sides. But as quickly as chaos had erupted, order was restored. Carmen had her arm around the radio girl: "*Cálmate, chica.*"

Meanwhile, Larry had gotten a grip on the baseball player's shoulders, and held them for a long moment with what must have been firm pressure. "George," he said quietly, and George's glee twisted out of his mouth. "You can put the bowl down now." When the bowl was settled back in its place, Larry said, "You can apologize to your parents now."

George shot a glance at a couple standing huddled together by the tree—the man looked a lot like him, only bald—who didn't seem surprised by George's behavior, just beaten down, tired. George stared at the floor with an expression of genuine, bashful remorse, but as Larry led him out of the room by the elbow, his last look back was mischievous, proud. I realized then that Sara had been squeezing my hand and was now shaking her head, saying, "Bad, bad." Carmen came over and stroked Sara's hair. These outbreaks probably always upset her.

"The Grab Bag's not for a little while yet," Carmen told her. "If you like you can take June upstairs to show her your room. Would you like that?"

Sara wiped the back of her hand across her mouth, smearing her lipstick a little. "*Gracias*, Carmen. Sara show her."

The stairs were covered with the same brown carpet as the living room, only the wall was white plasterboard, so full of scuff marks you'd think the people walked on that instead of the steps. Sara led me around a corner into a small bedroom with a window looking out on the street. The room was spotless and smelled of Lysol. I eyed the door to the closet across from the single bed, curious whether it still housed her collection. She led me by the hand to the bed. "Sit," she said. "Sara be right back. Sara get something to show June. Real nice."

I lay back on the bed, to rest for a minute. I was amazed, lying there, that I'd made it so long on my feet. I closed my eyes and let myself sink, then sat up so fast I got dizzy. Had I dozed? Everything suddenly seemed very quiet. How long had it been? Where was Sara? Maybe she'd gone to the bathroom. Maybe she'd fallen down. The room tilted when I stood up, but I stepped forward and reached for the doorframe. I should find her. I was responsible.

Down the long hallway, all the doors stood partway open. I felt like a thief looking in, but I scanned each room long enough to be sure it was empty. The light from the front windows had faded by the end of the hall, and when I turned the corner it was out of a virtual dark that he came: George, his overalls down around his knees, his hand on his penis. I didn't even know I'd made a sound until I heard the scream echo after me. I must have tripped in my rush down the stairs. I found myself on the floor, looking up at Larry and Carmen, whose eyes were not on me but on George at the landing, clutching his overalls at his waist.

"Where's Sara?" Carmen said.

"I don't know," I said. "I was looking . . ."

I stopped. Sara had appeared next to George, fingering the skirt of her dress as though her slip were bunched up underneath. She wore an expression I'd never seen on her face before—an almost sensual slackening. Carmen and Larry were now looking at me as if I had done something wrong. I stood up and held on to the banister. One of the fathers put his head through the living-room door. "Everything's fine. Go on back to the party," Carmen told him. Then to me: "Maybe you better go home now."

Sara's mouth looked swollen with her smeared lipstick. She smiled a distant, almost pitying smile down at me while I pulled on my raincoat, steeled myself for the cold, as if she were only sorry I had to leave early. The way Carmen ushered me to the door, I could have been one of the group-home people, her hand on my back careful with its authority.

The season can't seem to make up its mind. Last night a wet snow dropped like a sigh of relief on the city, and this morning, a row of great, dripping icicles curtains the cafe window. When the waitress brings my coffee, I thank her by name. My new apartment has a real kitchenette, but I come here a few times a week. My place faces the air shaft, so the cafe light is better for reading. I've been reading a lot since I quit the proofing job. I'm working only dinner shifts at the restaurant, and I try to use the days to improve myself, looking toward the time when I can settle on some kind of vocation. The cafe has a mirror along the side wall, to give an illusion of width, and I like to glance over at myself between paragraphs. Each time I see myself it's still a surprise. There's an intriguing opacity, as if I were looking at somebody else: the black-and-white herringbone spilling down the back of my chair, the short-cropped hair, tinged with burgundy, the purple sweater halfway to my knees. I don't go over to the East Village much, and when I do I steer clear of Fifth Street, the way you avoid an old lover's block, but I like to think that if I ever ran into anyone from the group home, they'd never know me, anyway. Sometimes I even imagine going back to the Binibon one afternoon, sitting at my old table.

The bells tinkle and Sara comes in. Her gaze rests on me, brightens at the new face. The smile hangs suspended on her mouth a minute. Maybe she's remembering that nice lady who used to sit there, that June. She smooths the quilting of her ski jacket over her chest. She touches her hair, to feel if the red barrette is in place. Then she takes the first step my way, her eyes as empty and hopeful as all new beginnings.

Pearlcorder

Some people try to save their marriage by having a baby. Some take a last-ditch trip and call it a second honeymoon. You got me this miniature tape recorder for our last anniversary. One more present that was really for you. We could use it for lists of things to be done, you said. Maybe then I'd get something accomplished.

In those days, before you left, you were the only one who talked into it. Even when you were hardly talking to me, you still spoke into the recorder. You hesitated after the plumber and garbage bags, then said an awkward 'bye, or cleared your throat and didn't say anything. But it's a voice-activated recorder. The machine stops when you stop. I never knew if the pause was as brief as it sounded or if you sat there for some time in between, wondering what had become of us.

Once you left I started playing your lists back, for a little company. I understood why you'd liked the voice activation. I bet you left the recorder on the whole time I slept and you were having your coffee. Your mind hit every now and then on some little thing I could do for you and you spoke, as if you weren't really speaking to a machine. The tape started moving as soon as it heard you, and died when you stopped. By the time you'd finished two cups, you'd have a whole list, efficient, encouraging. The most eloquent thing about what you said would have been the pauses. I hated those tight little tapes, like getting the third or fourth draft of a love letter. It didn't take very long to erase them. Then I started to use the recorder.

Maybe you didn't even know you could turn the voice-activation switch off. That's what I do. I speak now and then, when I feel like it. But what I'm also recording is the silence, all the particular silences of me in this house. I'm stockpiling batteries. I'm just keeping the recorder with me and running it. Running it at night in case I should talk in my sleep, or snore. Running it as though if it stops, I'll stop.

It's not that I'm trying to document my existence, like Dennis Hopper in *The American Friend*, shooting himself with a Polaroid until he falls back onto the pool table, covered with pictures of his own face at various stages of apparition. I don't play the tape back again and again, the way I pored over my teenage diaries, pretending I was someone else—a man—or that they were a novel. I use only one of the microcassettes. I don't bother to flip it. I just use one side and keep recording it over. I'm not looking back. I'm talking, I'm not listening.

The machine is a sleek little black number. It fits in the palm of my hand. I push the buttons like I was playing an instrument. I masturbate with one hand and hold the machine in the other, aiming the microphone to pick up my sounds. I don't look at myself when I do it. Sometimes I even think of you, you've become enough of a stranger. Sometimes I say dirty things, the way we used to when we first got started. Why is it that later it made us ashamed with each other? I must be ashamed when I say those things to myself. Isn't it the shame that arouses me?

I don't go out of the house very much lately, but when I do, I take the recorder along with me. Most of the time it just sits in my bag, but sometimes I hold it. I say a few things from time to time the way you might to a dog you were walking—cheerful things. I plan my little excursion, how I'll head to the park, then downtown for lunch. I'm only making a list. That's what you got it for in the first place. That's what I'm supposed to do with it. If I see someone walking down the block toward me, I drop the recorder back into my bag. It's small, okay, but someone might notice it. I say, I'm only making a list. I imagine the tiny wheels spinning behind their clear window.

I'm sure if you knew the way I was using it, you'd take the recorder back. You'd say that it was no good for me, it was holding me down, the way you said *you* were holding me down when you left me. I'm not worried. I can change whenever I want to. I've got an idea. What if I didn't say anything for such a long time that when I finally spoke my voice would be new? What if I put the machine on fast forward?

Stinking Benjamin

Trout Lily. You know why they call it that? Look at the leaves.
Mottled brown on a sea-green background, like some tenacious
memory of aquatic life right here on the forest floor. Today
is the first time this spring I've noticed them—no flowers yet,
just the pairs of small fishes—and suddenly, overnight, they're
everywhere, flashing their scales out from among last year's
dead. When I get back home, this is how I'll greet Mark:
proud and breathless with news of the Trout Lilies, an exclusive bulletin from my morning walk through the woods. But
for now, while I'm still alone, finding them also saddens me.
It's not just the inevitable nostalgia of seasons, but the fact
that wildflowers always remind me of Jan. *Trout Lilies are one
of the very first. Most people never see them at all. They don't
know what to look for.*

It's two years this winter since I moved up from the city
to work for the *Valley Tribune*, resigned to getting my start in
"the provinces." Jan did pen-and-ink illustrations for the paper, mostly for the nature and cooking columns. I can still
remember the first time I saw her come bounding into the
newsroom with her short red hair, flat chest and lavender
running shoes. She moved with an athleticism that was dis-
concerting in a newsroom of pasty-white reporters and editors,

who carried their extra ten pounds ceremoniously, like their press cards. It wasn't until she stopped at my desk to introduce herself that I got a closer look at her eyes, her hands, and realized she wasn't such a young woman. One of the other reporters said she was fifty, and sneered, as if to be fifty and drawing little pictures of mushrooms and birds and whole-grain breads was somehow less than respectable. Nobody seemed particularly fond of her. She had a high wheeze of a laugh and she talked too loud, so when she met with her editor, the rest of the staff shot each other knowing glances or rolled their eyes back in their heads. I didn't care. I needed a friend that winter.

I was renting a farmhouse on a back road, but the paper kept me so busy that for all the use I made of the woods and fields and trails, I might as well have taken an apartment in town. I went for a long walk the first really warm Sunday, though, and came back with a trophy: a bouquet of burgundy flowers, exotic as orchids, from the side of the road. I made a vase of a water glass and set it up on my night table, blooms impossibly rich and deep against the leaves' buoyant green— a small token of homeyness.

That Monday, Jan gave me a ride when my car got held up at the shop, and she instantly fell in love with the farmhouse: the barn where I didn't keep animals, the country kitchen where I never baked bread, the walk-in pantry, shelves empty of Mason jars. She started to zigzag with her long, proprietary strides room to room, saying I needed something for the walls, needed plants, imagining a bright rag rug in the hallway. She wanted to see my bedroom, and for a minute I hesitated, as if it were a man asking.

Stinking Benjamin. You've got to be kidding me. Jan pointed to my bouquet. *Don't you know what those are?*

I shook my head.

Smell them.

She shooed me over toward the night table, where I bent

to the flowers, expecting something evocative, sinfully sweet, like their shade, wondering that I'd never thought to smell them when I'd picked them. I must have made a terrible face at the odor. She laughed so hard I was afraid she would choke and I remembered, that morning, noticing something rotten in the air, too hurried to pay much attention.

Trillium, a.k.a. Stinking Benjamin, were beautiful but smelled like old garbage. Trout Lilies had delicate, curved yellow petals. In a couple of weeks the streambeds would be paved with Marsh Marigolds. *We've got to educate you city girls. What are you doing Saturday?*

Jan owned a little house in town with a tiny perimeter of yard, out of which she squeezed flower beds and the world's narrowest vegetable garden. Most of the time we got together at her place, not mine. Her small rooms were cluttered with drawings and photographs, scrolls of Japanese calligraphy, macramé hangings, clay pots—Jan went through crafts the way other single women might go through love affairs—and after a long day at the paper I liked to go there and let her show me things, loiter by the side of the stove while she basted chicken or stirred spaghetti sauce, drink her cheap wine.

She made a hobby of going to yard sales and used-clothing stores, and after dinner she'd take me upstairs to try on her latest finds. For herself, she was partial to almost anything purple, but she started to bring home other things with me in mind. She lay on her bed, propped up on an elbow, while I modeled flowered sundresses from the fifties, with full pleats and sculpted bodices; wool skirts so narrow I could barely get them up over my hips; lacy blouses and soft, beaded cardigans. When I asked her how much she'd spent, she always dismissed me with a wave of the hand that looked, from her reclining position, like some grand salon gesture. The dress had been a couple of bucks, the blouse three, or two-fifty, she couldn't remember. *Forget about it. Come lie down.* Then she'd reach back to the shelf by her bed for a carved wooden box and roll a joint of mostly seeds and stems, that seemed to work on us anyway.

Among the other mysterious containers and books on her shelf was the framed photograph of a young woman with shoulder-length, sandy-blond hair. One evening that summer I finally asked her about it. She picked up the picture and studied it, as if it were of someone at the same time very familiar and strange, the way I might look at a picture of myself from ten or fifteen years ago.

Jan had been married for thirteen years, down South, to an army sergeant. *Yes, sir. A regular housewife. Two kids. Station wagon, hair curlers, you name it.* She looked at me matter-of-factly while I worked to grasp the idea that she'd had this other existence, more than half my whole lifetime; while I tried to imagine my own mother off by herself, cooking dinner and buying clothes for some other young woman.

Jan's first child was Gillian, the young woman in the photograph. Her second was a boy, Wynn. The week before he would have turned seven, Wynn drowned in the lake half a mile from their house. Though Jan didn't say so, I gathered his death had unhinged her. When her husband filed for divorce three years later, Gillian, who was twelve by then, elected to stay with the sergeant. *Of course, that was the best thing for her. She needed structure. I can't imagine how she'd have survived in a nuthouse like this.* She put the picture back on the shelf and made a brittle attempt at a smile, shrugged her shoulders. But she didn't fool me. I didn't have to ask to know that her daughter had sent the picture but never once come to visit her.

Toward the end of that summer, I didn't see Jan for a couple of weeks. She was getting ready for a show of drawings and calligraphy at the local women's center. The night of the opening, seeing her was like seeing a lover I'd started taking for granted in the light of a circle of beautiful women. She wore a lavender crepe ruffled blouse from a fancy second-hand shop in Boston. Her skin was flushed pink under the gallery track lights. She held court by a table laid out with cheese and tea breads and wine, laughing, taking long sips from a mug, hugging and kissing a parade of women I'd never seen before. I wished I'd been the one to bring her the vase full of purple irises. I wanted to be her best friend, set apart from all the others buzzing around her with praise; wanted to make some intimate remark that would show my special claim on her.

That night I also looked at her work differently. Seeing her overstuffed folders of sketches, her closets opening to an avalanche of meaningless Japanese marks, I'd never thought too much about Jan as an artist. But another friend of hers made wooden frames, and Jan had been up nights for a week cutting mat boards. Lifted out of the chaos and dust of her rooms, encased in glass, smooth grains and squares of bright color, the simple strokes came together into a kind of poetry. A series of sleeping cats curled and stretched, elastic and languorous. I also liked the eggplants, the way Jan had made them look Japanese, the dark wash of purple. Finally the one I kept coming back to was almost the simplest: the figure in charcoal of a nude woman, bent at the waist and reaching down to her toes, the few strands that suggested her hair spilling over, the point of her breast like the ideogram of a sea gull in flight. It couldn't have taken more than a couple of minutes to execute, but it was perfect—pure abandon, a waterfall.

The better pictures were priced high, partly to make the whole thing look serious, partly because Jan didn't really want to part with them. But I was sure she'd give me a deal; I could pay in installments. She marked the card below the drawing of the woman with the red-dot sticker—Sold—but she didn't want money; she said we'd work out a trade. By the time I went home, Jan was giddy from jug chablis and success and I still hadn't figured out what I could offer in return for the drawing. But it didn't take her long. She called the next afternoon with her proposition: she'd give me the drawing—matted and framed—and I'd give her writing lessons. Even she had to admit she was getting old for her waitress job. She didn't make much selling her couple of drawings a week to the paper, but if she could write articles too, become one of the stringers . . . It seemed a fair enough trade. Jan said I should come over for dinner—she could see I'd gotten skinny while she'd been preparing her show—and afterward we could have our first lesson.

Jan bought a bottle of champagne and had found some real pot. It wasn't much of a lesson, but at least we planned our attack. She would go out and research a couple of articles. We'd work on outlines together and she'd write the first drafts. We'd coax the drafts into shape, and then she'd take the finished pieces in to the editor. When we poured the last of the bottle, we toasted Jan Lowe, Special to the *Valley Tribune*. My end of the bargain was going to be easy.

I can still see her racing into the newsroom that fall, the first day one of her stories appeared. She was wearing a blazer— I could tell it wasn't used, that she'd splurged on it—and carrying a lavender canvas briefcase. Her chin was a few inches higher than usual as she navigated the channel between desks toward the pile of first-run editions. The story was about a mother-daughter team who had opened a successful French restaurant, and though it was buried on page twenty-three, it wasn't too bad a spread. She'd gotten a decent photo of the two women smiling in their chef's hats, indistinguishable as the mother-daughter look-alike pairs in those dish-detergent commercials. Jan made her way toward my desk as she read it, head buried inside the paper, sure as the blind. But halfway over, she stopped short. Her face came out wild from behind the mask of the pages. The women's last name was misspelled in the photo caption. A few lines in the third paragraph were scrambled, and one whole paragraph was wiped out, as if she'd never written and rewritten it.

Things like that happened all the time at the *Tribune*, but Jan made noisy demands for retractions, corrections. She insisted on seeing the managing editor, and I could hear every word she said through his flimsy office partition. She'd proofread her stories herself if no one else cared enough to be accurate. And while they were on the subject, what was her article doing on page twenty-three when that wire-service drivel about a soap-opera star was plastered all over the feature page? Her face was crimson by the time she stormed out, but I noticed she didn't leave without grabbing a handful of papers.

I'd always assumed there would be a finite term to the lessons, but even when Jan was publishing enough to quit waitressing, she didn't seem to figure I'd paid off the picture. She didn't just want her stories printed, she wanted them to be *good.* Good enough that the stringers' editor wouldn't grimace whenever he saw that flash of carrot and lavender coming; good enough that they'd hire her, and not another college kid, when they had a staff opening. Jan had come a long way, to the point where there was nothing wrong with her writing, nothing you could put a finger on. But it didn't have that touch; it didn't have what she had with her wands of charcoal, her ink quills. I had it in my stories, or so people told me, but I didn't think about it; it just came. I could no more teach it to her than she could have taught me to draw those lightning, articulate curves that turned a few strokes into a woman's body.

We still got together at her place Tuesday nights. She made dinner, and at my insistence I brought the wine. But by the start of that winter, when we cleared the plates and glasses away, we didn't have a lesson so much as a gripe session. Jan wasn't paid enough for her articles. They never got good enough play. The editor always came up with such embarrassing headlines. She said they'd be sorry they hadn't treated her better when she was gone: Jan Lowe was launching a job hunt.

Every Tuesday when I arrived, she presented me with the latest version of her résumé, with some new euphemism for "secretary" or "substitute," some new set of headings or format, as if she could camouflage the basic fact that she was fifty years old and that in the desert of employment, she'd been a nomad.

She spent a lot of time that winter retyping the résumés, answering ads, donning her blazer and briefcase for interviews. But there was never any good news. I began to dread Tuesdays. What could I do but encourage her? Say, Sure, why not, apply. Say, It can't hurt to send them a letter. But Jan had gotten insatiable, grim. Drinking and smoking didn't make her fun anymore; it turned her stubborn, desperate. She looked at me from the other side of the table, over the pile of résumés and classified columns and article clippings, as if she weren't going to let me go until she had what she needed, something of mine—my prospects, my youth, as if those things were things I could give, as if I were holding out on her.

It's better to think about that Indian summer before everything changed, like that Saturday we'd been out all day, chasing fall leaves the way we'd hunted wildflowers. Our clothes were gray from the dusty dirt roads, and back at her house, Jan produced a couple of robes—purple velour for herself, for me a peach silk yard-sale kimono. She had Joan Armatrading's new album and she put it on, loud. We pushed the table and chairs to the edge of the dining room and started dancing. The air was warm and heavy, and even when we opened all the windows, beads of sweat tickled me inside the silk. Before long, we took off the robes and danced in our underpants—

Jan's leathery nipples stark against her tiny, girl's breasts, my fuller breasts swinging, the two of us singing "Me, Myself and I" at the top of our lungs.

When the record was over, we collapsed on the couch. In between hard breaths, she surprised me by speaking: *I always lose my best friends to men.* At that moment I wanted to swear it wouldn't be that way with me, to seal our friendship with some grade-school vow, like when two girls prick their fingers, squeeze them till they bleed and then rub them together.

Mark wasn't the reason I pulled away from Jan. He just made it easier.

Now, when I get back from my walk, on the morning of the first Trout Lilies, the house has a shut-up, sleeping look to it, and I imagine Mark turning over to my empty half of the bed, wrapping the quilt tighter around him. Across the road, the sun hasn't yet topped the line of maples. I pass the house and keep walking, into a stretch enclosed on either side by thick pines that guard a wintry dampness. In among the trees, I can make out grainy remnants of snow in the shadows, and the forest's sodden carpet gives off a dank, mulching smell. There is scant sign of spring here. Carefully as I look, the brown is not broken by even a tentative shoot of green, by anything hopeful and speckled.

It was in this same kind of endless annex to winter that I did the story on the office where Mark works. When he called to ask me out for a Tuesday-night movie, I looked at Jan's drawing hanging over my nightstand and told myself I had earned it: the tender fold of her belly, that lassitude of her hair; Jan's woman letting go, falling.

Mark and I stayed out late in a bar that first night. After a few drinks he started to tell me his plans—work here a couple of years, then move to the office in the state capital. Maybe direct a division, or go out on his own. He didn't seem to think it was premature to imagine me into his future. With another year or two at the *Tribune*, my reputation and background, I could easily land a job at one of the statewide dailies. It was strange to hear him say it, as though it would be nothing at all, only natural, and I realized that in all my months of listening to Jan, I'd started to hunker down to the limits of her horizons.

The second time I called Jan to cancel for a Tuesday night, she suggested we change our *appointment* to Thursdays. I actually got up the nerve to tell her: The lessons had gone on for almost eight months. I thought I had paid for the picture, and then some. For a moment there was silence over the line, before she said we should get together Thursday night anyway, and go to the movie downtown. I told her Mark and I had already seen it. Then she wanted to know about Saturday. She thought we could go for a walk in the woods. *It's a touch early still, but we might find some Spring Beauties.*

I didn't stop seeing Jan altogether, not right away. Every week or so I'd find time to stop by her house after work. But I started to feel like a visitor. When I remarked on her gardens, or the wall she'd spent the past weekend scraping clean of old paper, I could hear in my enthusiasm a false, solicitous ring. When we were together, we carried on two conversations that never met. She talked about the paper and jobs, and I talked about Mark. During her turn I half-listened, while someone inside me jumped up and down and shouted: It's not me. It's not my life.

If I went to Jan's from the office, I'd usually find her in the kitchen, simmering rice, chopping vegetables. She always seemed to have plenty for two, as if she'd been expecting me, but more and more I declined her invitations to stay, saying I had some food back at my place, had work to do. Once when I hadn't seen her for almost three weeks, I was coming home late past her house from the paper. Her car was in the driveway and there were lights in the windows, but when I tapped on the glass of her kitchen door, she didn't answer. I peered in to find her at the table under the tired yellow light, bending over a pile of newspapers, squinting through bifocals like an old woman. She never looked up. After a couple of minutes I crept back to my car and shut the door as if someone were sleeping.

That spring, I tipped Mark off about Trout Lilies; waited for his surprise as he knelt to inhale Stinking Benjamin; hunted for fiddleheads and baked them into a quiche. At the end of May, he moved in with me. We got a few books on gardens and planted one. In the evenings, I liked to go out with my hoe and police the rows for weeds, turn the warm soil over and over, then spread a darkening stain with the hose as night fell. I was always amazed when the green shoots rose up from the buried treasure of good intentions and seeds, when each vegetable came up different. Jan said I should stop over and see her garden—all her perennials were in bloom. I meant to, but the days hurried by: pole beans, cucumbers, broccoli.

The nights had been cool for a week when Mark and I heard the warning on the radio of September's first killing frost. The days were short enough by then that we had to bring a flashlight out to the tomato plants. We took turns, one aiming the beam, the other snipping the firm green fruit from the vine. I'd read in one of our books that tomatoes ripened faster indoors if you wrapped them in newspaper. Mark went down to the cellar for a stack of *Tribunes* while I imagined steaming vats of sauce, the pantry lined with jars glowing red through the winter. He worked much more quickly than I. Before I used a sheet of newspaper, I glanced at the articles, remembering when they'd been written, if they'd been controversial—all the effort and argument reduced to slender, disposable columns of type. I came across one of Jan's stories, about a woman who'd started a business, calendars and greet-

ing cards with photographs of local wildflowers. The sentences
flowed pretty well. I got through a few paragraphs before
Mark shot me a mock-harsh get-back-to-work look and the
words were lost around a tomato.

I'd scrubbed just about all the printer's ink off my hands
when the phone rang. It was Jan. We'd been wrapping tomatoes, I told her, and then the "we" stuck in my throat. She'd
told me once back in the spring that when you stopped saying "I," you were definitely *going under*. I told her "I" still
had all my winter squash on the vines, that I'd also left the
carrots, potatoes. But she hadn't called to chat about garden-
ing; she had some news. She was putting her house on the
market and moving to South Carolina. She'd been hired as
a reporter for a weekly newspaper.

I had all kinds of ideas for her going-away present—a field
guide to wildflowers of the South; one of those beautifully
bound blank journal books. I was sure she'd said she wasn't
leaving for a few weeks. But when I called to ask her out for
a farewell dinner, her phone had been disconnected. The
stringers' editor knew only that she was gone. No one knew
the name of the paper. She'd mentioned it when she'd called,
the paper and also the town, but for the life of me I couldn't
remember.

Of course there were things I could have done to find out:
asked around at the women's center for the people I thought
were her friends; tried to locate her real estate agent; looked
at the newspaper directory under weeklies for South Carolina
to see if any sounded familiar; even sent a card to each one—
there couldn't have been all that many. It's not too late even
now. Every month or so, when something like the Trout Lilies
reminds me, I resolve to find her, and then I see the two of us.

We're tracking a streambed, flanked on either side with
the hard green fists of fiddleheads barely out of the ground.
In another week, she says, we can come back and pick them.

Suddenly she's scurrying up the steep bank to our right, agile as a youngster. In her wake she trails brown landslides of leaves and streaks of dark, muddy hillside. I pant and slip and scramble and still can't keep up with her. When I get to the top, I find her breathing easily, kneeling to a tiny flower, white with a center of gold. She turns her face up into the light like a sorceress bent over some secret ingredient, fierce with pride and complicity: *Bloodroot*. Before I've even gotten my wind back, she's scratching the dirt. She pulls up a root and holds it before my eyes, triumphant, as if I know what it means. *It's like a lot of things, it doesn't flower for long.*

She snaps the root in two and it bleeds a red juice; breaks it again until the vegetable blood runs down her fingers. She laughs and smears some onto my cheek, and then we're both digging, touching each other, arms and faces, with the fresh war paint, falling backward, cackling into the wind.

For Solo Piano

It was hard enough to stay celibate and sane without that sonata, that absolute symphony, of desire and attainment issuing forth from the upstairs apartment. What gave that pair of screamers the right to shatter the relative silence of apartment propriety, where the only intrusion of other lives on her own was the remote flush of a toilet, the bass heartbeat of a stereo a few floors above or below, a cough in the night, a natural shifting of floorboards?

She lived in one of those midtown, middle-rent high-rises where no one smiled or said a word in the elevator, no one so much as made eye contact, where people maintained an exterior sameness like that of their identical one-bedroom apartments. She had come to depend on that sameness to give her, by way of contrast, a sense of character. She took a certain pleasure in riding down to the lobby on Saturdays wearing her most disreputable jeans, in lighting a joint and watching the smoke trail up to the vents, imagining it filtered through the atmosphere of some middle-aged businessman's bedroom.

She covered her walls with museum posters. Her record collection was overflowing its cabinet. She grew house plants the size of trees, training their trunks into helixes. But there were days, in the midst of this accumulation, when what stood out about her existence was its entrenched, its unrelenting single-ness. The last thing she needed was new neighbors upstairs.

On an evening like any other, she took a long, circuitous stroll to watch the rush hour ebb, the dusk thicken, the lights come on. Then she set about selecting her dinner with the freedom and anarchy of those who don't have a soul waiting at home for them. She walked up to the Eighties for bread and wine, then east to First Avenue for fresh spinach pasta. She was friendly with the shopkeepers, so by the time she arrived at her building with her arms full of packages, she'd exchanged a few smiles and remarks on the weather and gotten some slim sense of human intercourse. She'd barely come in, dropped her bags on the counter and taken her coat off, when the neighbors gave her their first serenade.

It was a muted cry that she first took for a child's but then recognized as more articulate, almost a word, an incantatory monosyllable, like *yes* with a strong current of breath in it. The sound was clearly coming from right overhead, yet it had this quality of surrounding her, of emanating from the very walls, of being almost inside her apartment. She stared amazed at the ceiling, mute as any other these past couple of years, as if she expected whoever it was to fall through and land at her feet in a downpour of plaster. Then the sound switched to something like a musician practicing scales along progressively higher octaves, four or five ascending notes, then dropping down to begin the rise again, starting with a pleading tone and ending with more of a thank-you, but provisional, that needed more, needed always and again to start over.

She shook herself when she realized how she'd been listen-ing. The idea was to ignore it. It's got to end sooner or later, she said to herself, moving back to the kitchen, unpacking her dinner fixings with a tremendous rustling of bags, a crackling of cellophane. But the sounds caught her up again in a mo-ment when the man joined in with a counterpoint, a low, distended, muscular tone that wove in and out of the woman's scale of cries, that were shortening to a staccato.

Each time the woman trembled at the top of the scale, each time the man took his closing sweep downward, she figured surely that was the resolution. But she'd sigh and start to climb again, he'd suck in a loud breath, they'd pause for an instant (a kiss?) and then burst forth as if out of a long suffocation.

She didn't like to eat alone in restaurants. She could go home every night of the week, concoct her gourmet dinner for one—complete with wine, candlelight, music—and six nights out of seven feel no acute deprivation. But exile her into this mirrored Second Avenue cafe and all that she noticed was couples. Heads leaning together across daisies in Perrier bottles. Elbows sliding together over Plexiglas tabletops. Soundless syllables quavering between two pairs of lips like some sympathetic vibration.

It wasn't as if she hadn't had her share of love, in what she now thought back on as the late, extended adolescence of her early twenties. She'd produced those sighs and moans that are a subtle orchestration of sound effects toward the convenient crescendo, and seemed to work surprising effects on her lovers, who believed for all the world they were coaxing it out of her. And, she had to admit, there were those few times she'd forgotten and the sound had continued to well out of some place deeper than her throat, some rarely tapped, genuine ardor; when she'd heard an actual wail in a pitch she'd never have recognized as her own.

Say you're a woman going on thirty and, for better or worse, hopelessly heterosexual. Say you move to Manhattan from your midwestern hometown, with the intention less of finding a man than of escaping your mother's obsession with your finding one. Her twice-weekly phone calls. Her timid ques-

tions. Her peddling your number to this one's son, that one's
nephew, who was a doctor or in business, and never called
anyway. Say you've been, to use the phrase of every solicitous
aunt in Illinois, not much blessed in love. Say you've devel-
oped a private mythology about the mysteries of coupling.
The single woman must not spend her time seeking men,
even thinking about them, but rather must turn her energies
to self-enhancement. Move to New York. Find a well-paying
administrative/clerical position with a mid-sized company.
Join a health club. Take a routine satisfaction in scrubbing,
combing and clothing yourself so you're not unattractive but
almost entirely functional. Then, in defiance of a certain
logic, the more you filled your days, the more you'd feel a
new kind of space opening inside you, a place that could be
less need than an ampleness, a sort of spare room that meant
you were ready to let someone in.

It had happened for her, though not exactly that way. The
place that opened felt more like a hunger, a bottomless, general desire, a perpetual state of anticipation, as if there were
this person who was always almost in sight, slipping around
the next corner, disappearing down subway stairs, going the
other way through the next turnstile. The kind of unobjecti-
fied longing that made her react to a pathos in even the stu-
pidest top-forty love songs and search the faces of passersby in
a way you shouldn't do in the city.

Yet this place that had opened could also heal over. It had
been long enough now that the desire that had been so great
was shrunk to a small, inward sadness, like a sprig of lace on an
undergarment no one else is going to see. She tried not to in-
dulge the idea that this was one more step in her preparation,
only a longish prelude. She sat in the cafe with an asparagus
salad and a good Chardonnay and thought about how maybe
this was the whole song.

It was past midnight by the time she went home. After dinner she wandered down through the abandoned, semicom-

mercial blocks of the Thirties, then came back uptown for
another glass of wine in one cafe, a cup of tea in another. She
figured at some point they'd have to exhaust themselves.
When she got to the door of her apartment, she turned the
key with stealth and a certain agitation, as if she would surprise them in her own bed, as if the sound would burst out at
any second. She listened and heard the ticking of a clock.
Someone sneezing. She dropped her clothes in a trail across
the bedroom rug and crawled gratefully under the quilts, as
if perhaps all that had been her imagination.

Sometime toward dawn she was doing a variation on that
old girlhood dream, the one all her friends confessed they'd
had too. She was at her desk in the office and everything was
perfectly ordinary except that she had no clothes on, only
these vampy, spike-heeled sandals. She was so aware of her
nakedness, so uncomfortable, yet also strangely excited; but
no one else seemed to notice it. The boss called her into his
office to take some dictation and she was paralyzed at the pros-
pect of leaving the shield of her desk, crossing the floor of the
office. Just then she was saved, she was awakened, by the
neighbors' lovemaking.

Floating in a kind of preconscious relief, she didn't fight the
sounds as they crested, broke overhead. She listened to every
note of the song in that waking liberation from guilt, that con-
fusing arousal. She was the woman. She rose and trembled at
each precipice of the other's desire, she heard each of the
man's long notes as him inside of her. When at last the resolution came, she fell back, the covers sloughed off, a damp
tingle across her skin: that forgotten sensation.

The elevator ride was worse than usual the next morning.
She didn't know whether it was harder not to blush or not to
smirk, a sort of I-know-you-know-I-know situation. She kept
to herself as much as she could at the office, flashing occa-
sionally on those sandals, the way the path from her desk to

the boss's had seemed like a long, narrow stage, lined with footlights. Around the middle of the afternoon she started to get drowsy, almost outright nodded off at her desk, as if she hadn't slept well at all but had been half-awake all night, waiting for them to get started. She went straight home at five. She didn't need to stop anywhere. Cautiously but with a forced confidence she put on slippers, opened a bottle of wine, started to break out the pasta, all the while with an ear toward the ceiling, almost sheepishly, with an awkward mixture of dread and anticipation.

They didn't come home until much later, after she'd had dinner and most of the wine, listened to music for violin and piano, piano and saxophone. It was a perfectly wonderful evening except that the silence of the place seemed so fragile, the time so conditioned by the fact of waiting. And she felt again that space inside her, but felt it like a violation, like shame, as if these two absolute strangers had come and ripped off a door she had carefully sealed. She was sitting in the middle of her queen-size bed, surveying it like some vast and desolate geography, when she heard them.

The sound of their key in the door brought with it an unexpected relief. If the couple upstairs had reopened this gap in her life, they were in a funny way also filling it. So now she sat, poised for an outburst of giggling, shrieks, a kicking off of shoes, a flinging of garments. Yet she heard nothing more than a faucet running, a flush. After a time she could make out a low murmur of conversation, which might have been some gentle prelude except it sounded so sober and toneless, so unlike anything she could imagine those two would say to each other. And then she could swear she heard the smack of an utterly passionless kiss, the kind that wasn't a prelude to anything—a punctuation. How was this possible? She trained her ear as close as she could to the ceiling and detected a stereo rustling of bedcovers, the winding of a clock, and then the accustomed silence of the apartment-house

night. She fell asleep like that, listening to forty-five floors of
such minute nocturnes.

After another couple of quiet nights, it came to her that
there was a plausible explanation for everything. The rightful
tenants must have gone off on a midweek business trip and
given the key to some desperate friends, who seized their few
hours of forbidden ecstasy. When she fell asleep, she dreamed
a piece of music without resolution: a jazz pianist, drunk but
still brilliant, playing the same tune with endless, subtle chord
changes into the night. It may be that a particular note in
her was struck toward morning—a key of resignation, some
cadence of hope. So when she woke, she wasn't sure whether
something in her had died or been born, if a song had been
found or forgotten.

Eating Air

When the ride got bumpy over the Adirondacks, Rachel's hand automatically reached for the bakery box, strapped in on the seat next to hers. She'd been traveling with the box for so many hours, it had become a sort of companion. Maybe like traveling with a sleeping baby, she thought—the way you'd instinctively check, touch, adjust it. She smiled to herself, imagining Susan's face when she saw her coming in through the gate with the outsized white box, held ceremonially in front of her. For the umpteenth time she pictured the towering creation inside, mentally crossing her fingers that the moats and turrets of meringue cream hadn't gotten mashed by the box top, that the green candied cherries still sat primly aloft on each turret. The most extravagant Key Lime Pie on Miami Beach, the paper's veteran food writer had assured her. God knew what the thing tasted like, but it was a vision. A fantasy, a confection, like the Beach itself—those mint and flamingo and ice-blue pastry palaces she still couldn't get over, even though she'd been there now almost a year. On weekend afternoons, when she wasn't stuck working over a story, she'd smoke a joint and stroll along Art Deco Row: the pastel towers rising unreal into the air and on the ocean side, a punctuation of palms and the blue blue beyond, and each vision appeared equally artificial, something you could marvel at but never join.

The airplane began its descent. She wasn't sure if the drop was making her stomach queasy, or if she was nervous. For the first time it struck her that Susan might not recognize her right off. It had been four years, and Rachel was thinner now; she'd cut her hair short and traded in her perennial myopic glaze for a pair of Lucite-framed eyeglasses. She couldn't imagine Susan looking any different, even though she knew having a baby could change you. She got a flash of the picture she still kept on her bulletin board of the two of them in front of the freshman dining hall: Susan with that curly auburn hair Rachel had always envied, fiery corkscrews against the backdrop of ponderous marble; Rachel's straight brown hair tucked up under the black fedora that was her trademark that year. It always seemed to Rachel, when she studied the picture, that Susan had something complete about her; a kind of light to her face that lifted her more out of the moment, a steady, underlying light that would always be there. In contrast, her own image had a tentative, unformed look, as if when she'd turned to the camera, some great, baffling question had just occurred to her.

She kept a hand on the box through the final approach and landing, and stepped gingerly into the aisle and down the ramp. She'd gone to the Miami airport right from the office, in heels and a dress. The Vermont evening air was dry and cool, and it rushed up her legs with a pleasantly chilling sensation she associated now with air conditioning. She scanned the faces lining the aisle at the gate, but there was no sign of Susan. It was easy to imagine why she'd be late. Probably at the last minute she'd had to feed the baby, or change her. Rachel walked the length of the terminal, out and back, to be sure. In spite of herself, the fact that Susan wasn't there set her on edge. Wasn't it always Susan who'd cared a little less, made a little less effort? During the years after college, when they'd gradually drifted apart, wasn't it always Susan who stopped writing back, who never saved enough money to visit? She heard Susan's voice again, over the phone, when Rachel called to say she wanted to come to Vermont. Susan had said sure, but there was a hesitation, even a touch of panic, as if Rachel were some relative you didn't particularly like but couldn't say no to. With that thought, Rachel felt some of the old bitterness seeping back. Suddenly she hated herself for having been so excited, for traveling all that way. And the bakery box: big as it was, it looked pitiful sitting there on the empty row of chairs in the almost-deserted airport. Certainly carrying that ornate wedding cake of a pie all the way from Miami had been overdoing it.

She stared at the box as if it were the pie that had let her down. Then she succumbed to her curiosity. She slipped a clear-lacquered nail under the three strips of Scotch Tape, took a breath and slowly lifted the lid. A miracle: the pie was absolutely untouched, perfect as the plaster model in the bakery window. She peered in around the four sides to be sure. The sight of the candy green on the mountain of white re-assured her. *Of course it keeps,* she could hear the old Jewish baker snap at her. *They got refrigerators yet where you're going?* She admired the pie another minute, then tucked the flaps of the lid carefully back inside. Just then, she sensed someone standing behind her. She turned, relieved, all ready to forgive. But it wasn't Susan. It was a man.

"Rachel?"

"Hank?"

Susan hadn't said much about her husband in the couple of letters they'd exchanged since Rachel had resurrected their correspondence, but that was typical. On the subject of men, Susan had to be drawn out. She'd never felt the need to describe her boyfriends the way Rachel did, circling around and around those awful adjectives (*gorgeous, great-in-bed*) with anecdote after anecdote, as if she could convince Susan and

herself that this time it was really different, *deep*. *You'll just have to meet him*, Susan had said on the phone when Rachel started up with her questions. *You'll see when you come.*

Hank was skinny, but strong-looking in a wiry sort of way. He had tight brown curls cut short to his head, like one of those bathing-cap wigs the older women wore to her apartment-house swimming pool. There was an angry look to the arc of his eyebrows, the tight set of his mouth. "Susan was too tired to come get you," he said. It sounded like an accusation. "Aja kept her up last night."

"I wish she'd left a message with the airline." She tried to sound conciliatory. "I could have taken a cab."

"You can't take a cab to our place," he said. "This isn't the city." He stood there looking at her with an air of impatience. "You ready to go?"

She said sure, then remembered the bakery box. She picked it up self-consciously, but Hank didn't seem to give it much notice. He didn't ask if she needed help carrying anything, either. Between the box and the big weekend bag bouncing against her hip, she had to work to keep up with him as they crossed the parking lot. He had a beige Subaru station wagon, with an infant's car seat strapped in up front. Apparently it didn't occur to him that he might move it, so Rachel set herself up in back. The night was moonless and dark, and once they turned off the main road, all she could see was a tunnel of trees, great and full, materializing in front of the headlights. It seemed so long since she'd seen real trees—palm trees weren't real; they were stylized, decorative, a kind of vegetable flamingo—that for the first few miles she just stared out the window. Then she looked across at Hank. His shoulders and neck were muscle-bound, tense; he drove with both hands gripping the steering wheel.

"You know, it always amazes me that Susan wound up in Vermont," she said. "We took a trip up here together. Fall of senior year."

She waited, but Hank didn't speak.

"Did she ever tell you about it?"

He shook his head. He didn't look the least bit interested, but Rachel kept on; it felt good to break up the silence.

"We borrowed this old VW from a friend of ours. We weren't even sure the car would make it. We got up here on a Friday night and found a motel room." She stopped a minute, remembering the sense of triumph she and Susan had felt, seeing the motel lights from I-91 and screeching off at the exit, pulling in just in time to get the very last room. "The next morning, we looked out the window and we couldn't believe it—the colors."

She paused to think of how to describe them, but she glanced over at Hank and lost heart. They drove in silence for a few minutes. She decided to try a different approach, one she used with interview subjects—to break the ice with something neutral, impersonal. She steeled herself before she spoke. "So what's all this we're driving through?"

"This right here?" He turned to consider her for a moment, then went back to the road. "Mostly cornfields. Pastureland."

All Rachel could make out in the dark was ghostly suggestions, and now and then a great, hulking dairy barn, rising up and slipping past in its confident halo of electric light. She kept her eyes out the window, exaggerating the gesture to cover her awkwardness. But in a minute Hank spoke up again. "Up the hill to the left—that's one of our latest projects."

"Oh, really?" The enthusiasm rang false in her ears, but she nodded and craned her neck to peer into the dark hillside. Hank was a partner in New England Retrofit, a small company that remodeled old farmhouses with skylights and sunrooms and solar collectors. She couldn't see a thing, but she imagined a cross between an old barn and one of downtown Miami's reflective glass skyscrapers.

There was another long stretch of silence before the Subaru turned, nosing down into a deep rut, then muscling up a rise along a narrow dirt byway. She gripped the bakery box and tried to level it by angling her knees. He turned again, and pulled to a stop. Behind the trees, she could make out the sprawl of the farmhouse, and she heard barking. "Susan didn't tell me you had a dog."

"That's Mies. For Mies van der Rohe."

She gave him a funny look. It was a strange name for a dog—just as it was odd to name your baby *Aja*, after an old Steely Dan album. He apparently took the expression as a sign of ignorance on her part, because he added with a scarcely masked condescension, "The architect."

She followed him along a screened-in porch that was obviously one of his renovations. She took a tentative step over the threshold into the house itself. The creature arrived like an invisible force field out of the dark interior. Before she could move aside it leaped up at her, a humid wave of orange fur and breath, and landed with one paw on the pie box.

"Down!"

She felt a hairy slapping against her bare legs. She tried to move forward, but something yanked out from under her heel and the dog let out a high screech.

"You're stepping on Mies."

"Oh. Excuse me."

She was instantly sorry she'd let that slip out. Hank flipped the hall switch, and under the light she could see his face again, his almost frightening glare. But then she looked down at the box. The side where the dog had landed was completely bashed in. She held it up in front of his face, as though she didn't need to say anything further in her own defense.

He lifted his eyebrows: somewhere between a shrug and a halfhearted concession. "What's in there, anyway?"

"What's in there is a pie I've been carrying all the way from Miami."

He winced and put a finger up to his lips.

She followed him into a large kitchen, carrying the pie like

She set it down on the butcher-block ... nose of the dog, a ... air and wagging ... some treat for him. Hanging from a rack above the counter was a family of heavy black cast-iron skillets, and the wall beyond was floor-to-ceiling shelves that looked like something out of a health-food store: row upon row of Mason jars filled with dark-speckled flours, oddly shaped grains and beans and cereals, spices and teas. It hit her even before she opened the box and saw his face that she'd made a mistake.

The damage inside wasn't as bad as the state of the box had suggested. About a quarter of the meringue cream was mashed against the box top, but the rest was more or less spared. Hank looked on from a distance. "Didn't Susan tell you she doesn't eat refined sugar?" He stared at the pie like a vegetarian contemplating a slab of raw meat.

Rachel thought of the giant Toblerone bars Susan had brought back from her semester in France, of their two A.M. Dunkin Donuts runs. "No. She didn't happen to mention that."

Hank sighed, as if he were faced with a toxic-disposal problem in his own kitchen. Even the dog had backed off. Maybe he didn't eat sugar either. But all of a sudden he started prancing and wagging his tail. It was Susan, wrapped up in a plaid flannel bathrobe, several sizes too big. The way she stood there rubbing her eyes, she looked like a little girl in her father's robe. But when she dropped her hands down from her face, Rachel saw a more adult exhaustion around her eyes, tugging at the sides of her mouth.

"Ray," Susan said.

Rachel smiled. She'd forgotten the nickname. Only now it sounded dull, a statement of the fact of her presence, empty of the old teasing lilt. Still, this was it, the reunion, and she opened her arms. Susan moved sleepily toward her, and didn't so much hug her as let herself be hugged. Rachel held on to her a moment anyway, registering the bulk of her definitely swollen breasts, the faintly milky smell that rose out of the robe.

"Sorry I didn't come," Susan said. "Last night was a killer." She looked at Hank. Then her eyes alighted on the bakery box.

"It's Key Lime Pie," Rachel said, and shot Hank a severe look. "Supposed to be the best in Miami."

Susan shook her head. "You carried it all the way?" She patted Rachel's arm, less by way of thanks than of consolation. "We'll have to clear a space in the fridge for it," she said, starting to rub her eyes again.

"It's cool enough," Hank said, not meeting Rachel's eyes. "I'm sure it can keep till morning."

"Put it up somewhere Mies won't get it," Susan said.

"Right."

Hank closed the lid, pushing down the tabs with less care than he might have. When he lifted the box to the top of the refrigerator, Rachel thought she heard the pie sliding on its cardboard foundation. She almost called out, "Careful," but checked herself.

Susan led Rachel up to a guest room with old flowered wall-paper, a futon on the floor, and Susan's college collection of Impressionist posters. She hung just inside the doorway while Rachel settled her things—looking guilty, Rachel thought, but too tired to make amends. Finally Susan said, "We'll have lots of time tomorrow to talk."

Rachel nodded. "Sure. We've got the whole weekend."

Susan's footsteps receded, creaking, to the far end of the hall. Rachel listened to the muffled sound of whispering from the far room. When that died down, the rasping of crickets took over, enormous and taunting in the still night. She was used to the sound of walking radios, of cars with busted mufflers racing down the night streets; used to all the little, intimate apartment-house noises. But how was she going to sleep with those crickets? For the moment it didn't matter; she was absolutely awake. As she sat there, she couldn't help thinking how differently she'd imagined the start of the visit. She'd pictured them making a pot of coffee and sitting up into the early morning, talking and talking, as if you could make up four years in one night. Then the two of them, trying not to giggle, trying barely to breathe, tiptoeing into the baby's room. Susan would pull back the crib quilt, and even in the dark Rachel would be able to tell that she was beautiful, an angel sleeping . . .

On the way to the guest room, Rachel had noticed another, closed door that must be Aja's. She got up and walked quietly to that door, put an ear to it. She imagined for a moment that she could hear a tiny rhythm of breathing, but with the crickets it was impossible to be sure. She listened again, and even put a hand on the knob, but then thought better of it. What if she woke her?

Back in her room, she remembered the few joints she'd tucked into her toilet bag, hoping to corrupt the young mother. It felt like being home on college vacations: sliding the window painfully up the old tracks, wincing at the sound of the match lighting, drawing in and counting to sixteen, then watching the first long hit disappear through the screen into the black night, flicking the ash into the tray of the windowsill. She hadn't intended to, but she smoked most of the joint. The crickets seemed less insistent by the time she finished, but the silence inside the sleeping house was heavy, like a thickening of air, and Rachel felt curiously cut adrift, not just from the life of this house but from her own life, the length of the Eastern Seaboard away. She thought of Tony, the police reporter she'd been seeing the last few months; the hollow feeling she had on Sunday mornings when he'd slept over at her place and she didn't want to be waking up with him, seeing his we've-got-the-whole-day-ahead-of-us face.

Would Susan understand that she kept him around just to have someone to go with to newspaper parties, just to have sex with once or twice a week so she'd feel alive inside her pumps and professional dresses? Would Susan understand that after all her hopeful lunch dates and after-work glasses of wine, none of the women at the paper had become more than acquaintances?

Rachel shivered. The room had grown suddenly chill. She eased the window down and stood swaying for some moments, letting the stoned weight sift down out of her head. It hit her that she was terribly hungry. She slipped by the baby's door and stepped carefully down the stairs, feeling sneaky, and stupid for feeling it. In the kitchen, she glanced wistfully up at the pie box, which she only now realized shared its perch with a plastic garbage pail.

Along the top row of shelves, she found a few packages of rice cakes, and brought one down. She opened the outer plastic bag and the inner crinkly wrapping, growing less cautious with the promise of sustenance, and took out a cake. A kind of oversized cracker, she decided. She took a bite. The crunch exploded in her ears, but nothing in the house stirred, so she kept chewing.

The first cake disappeared before she was sure whether it had any taste or not. She took up a second and told herself it was a chocolate-chip cookie, a doughnut. She remembered the first diet she'd ever gone on, at age twelve. It had been summer then too, and all the kids on the block had lined up every afternoon at the Mr. Softee truck. Rachel had walked to the other end of the block, where no one would see her. She'd cupped her right hand in front of her and pictured the cone cradled there, the spiraling peak of soft chocolate custard. She would admire it for a moment before she started to take long, savoring licks, to police phantom drips down the cone, to run her tongue across the inevitable chocolate mustache. By the time she was chewing the airy waffle of the cone, she'd convinced herself she felt full. Nothing like Mr. Softee on a hot summer's day, she'd told herself.

Eating air. It was the same thing with these rice cakes. Without even thinking, she went through half the pack. She wasn't full, but she'd come down some. She put the rest on the shelf and crept back upstairs. Before she got to the guest-room door, she stopped. Was it in her head, or was it the baby, coughing and calling out a gurgly syllable?

When Rachel came to, she didn't know where she was. She remembered half-waking through the night to unfamiliar cries and folding them into her dreams, so they became someone calling her, calling and calling, but she didn't know how to answer. She sat up, and her eyes cleared to the vision of Renoir's lawn party, transporting her back to the series of rooms she and Susan had shared. She tried to hold on to the mood that washed in with the memory, a sense that everything was before her, possible; but she was in Susan's guest room, unbelievably it was almost ten years later, and what settled out was a feeling of exile, a hazy intuition of loss. The morning was quiet, except for a passing conversation of crows. Through the curtainless window, the sky was an easy gray—comforting but somber after Miami's unrelenting light. Stepping into the hallway, she sensed right away that no one was home. Still, she called out, "Susan?" and listened to how uncertain her voice sounded.

The door to the baby's room was open, and she stopped at the threshold, but didn't step in. It was all set up, impeccably adorable, like a store display: the little futon on its wooden frame, the miniature down quilt, the system of open white shelves with their foam shapes and fat-paged cardboard books, the stack of wooden doughnuts. A mobile of origami birds was suspended from the ceiling by almost invisible threads, and a soft, even shine settled over everything from the skylight above—no doubt courtesy of New England Retrofit. Being

there, spying into the room, Rachel found the fact of Susan's
baby scarcely more palpable than it had been when she'd gotten the letter. Married, just gave birth to a girl: she could
hardly believe it. Even though she and Susan had been out
of touch for three years, what stabbed her first—more than
even surprise—was a sense of betrayal. Susan had gone and
done this without consulting her? What sank in next was a
feeling that she'd been deceived, not so much by Susan as by
time, by her own sense of it—the way it seemed that as she
was moving forward, everything else would stand still, would
wait for her. But now this enormous breach had opened between her life and Susan's. Rachel was twenty-nine, but for
her, marriage and babies still lay safely in a future that receded
year by year even as she got older, just as the benchmarks of
her career aspirations receded. She'd never thought much
about it, never seen the eternal postponement as a sign of
some possible failure or lack, until Susan's letter.

The paper birds shifted and fluttered in a breeze that swept
in from the window. Rachel watched them for a minute, then
looked away. Her head was starting to throb. She needed a
cup of coffee.

Downstairs on the kitchen counter was a note: *Glad you're
getting some sleep. Out for a short walk. Help yourself to
breakfast,* with a single, wilting purple wildflower laid across
the bottom in place of a signature. Rachel ransacked the refrigerator, the freezer, the cabinets. No coffee of any kind. Not
even a jar of instant on hand for emergencies. And this could
be one. The weight over the top of her skull was starting to
press more insistently. She tried the shelves again, but there
wasn't even any black tea. They'd have to drive into town.
Even if it took half an hour.

Outside, the air felt mild and flat, almost an absence of
temperature. In the daylight she could get a better look at the
house: the blue clapboards embedded with cool, faceted
jewels of glass; the epidemic of daylilies; the two-seated lawn

swing under a mantle of apple trees. She pictured Susan and Hank in the swing, gliding back and forth to some private rhythm, talking in low tones that would reach across the lawn to Rachel only as an intimate hum, a conversation whose drift she wouldn't catch but that she would know excluded her.

She guessed they'd walked up the dirt road that dipped and rose and then disappeared into woods; but when she heard voices, they came from the opposite direction. In a minute, Mies was bounding up to the driveway wagging his tail, nuzzling his slimy dewlaps into her knees. Susan was carrying the baby at her chest in a blue corduroy Snuggly-pack. Sure enough, peeking out around a white bonnet were a few fine carroty wisps.

"Sleeping Beauty," Susan said, wiping her ever-wayward curls off her forehead. "You find breakfast?"

Hank stood to the side. Rachel smiled at him, hoping to make a better start than she had the previous night. He just nodded. She bent to look at what was visible of the baby's pink face, and reached a tentative hand up to the corduroy. She touched it, but only with enough pressure to feel that there was a body inside, that it was real. She looked from Susan to the baby and back. "Listen, I hate to say this, but I need some coffee."

"You know, I thought you were probably still drinking coffee," Susan said. "But then I totally spaced it out." She looked timidly over to Hank, as if his input were needed on everything. She asked if Rachel needed it right away.

Rachel glanced hopefully toward the Subaru. "Sort of."

Aja had to be changed before they could go into town. Rachel followed Susan upstairs to the bathroom. The baby began to stir as Susan lifted the Snuggly straps from her shoulders and lowered her down to the bathroom rug. When her perfectly blue eyes opened, they seemed to open onto Susan alone, as if the whole rest of the room, including Rachel, were just a hazy border surrounding her field of vision. She was wearing a white T-shirt with a cow on it, and the world's tiniest pair of red sweat pants. All of Susan's movements grew diminutive, fitting the scale of the tiny person lying there, kicking her tiny sneakered feet. With a few gentle tugs, the row of snaps on the inside seam of the pants fell open, revealing the diaper, the chubby, cream-white skin of the thighs. A zip of the tape on each side of the diaper and Susan crooned, "What a lovely poopie this morning."

Rachel didn't turn her head away fast enough to miss the impossibly golden impasto. She took a few steps back toward the door.

Susan turned. "Ever see a baby's poop before?"

Rachel shook her head.

"Isn't the color amazing?"

Susan turned back to the baby before Rachel could answer, slipped the diaper out from under her legs, whispering, "Aja." She slid it off the rug toward where Rachel was standing, reaching a hand up to cover her mouth and nose. Susan twisted around again to look at her. "Silly." She laughed. "It doesn't smell. Didn't you know that? It doesn't smell as long as they're only breast-feeding."

Rachel dropped her hand, but she was skeptical. How could something that looked like that *not smell*? Maybe it didn't bother Susan. Maybe if you had a kid, even its shit was a part of you.

Susan had Aja's two feet in one hand, in the air, while the other slowly cleaned the golden smear from the baby's bottom and thighs. She reached for a small bottle and squeezed out an orange oil down the crack of Aja's bottom. The baby wriggled, made a high, gurgling sound. "Yes. That tickles," Susan said. Now a faint smell did reach Rachel's nose, an almondy, blossom smell.

In a minute, Aja was rediapered and dressed. "Now you're all clean and new, aren't you?" Susan picked the child up, swung her up toward the ceiling and brought her down for a kiss. Aja squealed with delight, reached a little hand out to grab Susan's face. Then Susan pulled herself out of it, as though she'd only just remembered Rachel was standing there. "Okay. Coffee time."

Susan moved the car seat so she could sit in back with the baby. Rachel took the passenger seat, next to Hank. The day was turning a darker gray, and Hank said there was a chance of thunderstorms. Rachel almost looked forward to the possibility. Maybe a storm would dispel the tension she felt building inside her as they drove past mile after mile of farmland and woods, so dense a green you could suffocate. Only Susan kept up her chatter from the back seat. "Cow. Can you say 'cow'? Doggie. Like Aja's doggie."

Hank pulled to a stop in a small village that hung together for one longish block. He parked and said he had some errands to run. He'd pick up some coffee for back at the house, and meanwhile they could go have something at the cafe. "That way you two can have some time to talk."

Rachel was glad Hank would be leaving them, but she didn't like the way he emphasized the word *talk* and looked at her, as if he had an idea she had something particular she needed to talk about, as if Susan had told him she had *problems*.

The Bristol Center Natural Bakery had a half-dozen tables and a broad window ledge, filled with overgrown plants and political leaflets. Rachel tried not to sound in too much of a hurry when she asked for the coffee. Susan ordered a cup of raspberry tea. Aja started to fret and pull at Susan's shirt and Susan lifted it, fumbled with her bra. There was a man a couple of tables over, but Susan didn't seem to care. Rachel couldn't help staring: that beautiful, freckled breast ballooned out; the nipple gone leathery. She forced her eyes away, up, but Susan's face was no less dangerous: the way her gaze fixed on Aja with that unspeakable tenderness, the way everything in her face seemed to be letting go, opening.

"So what does it feel like?"

Susan thought for a minute. "You know, it's almost sexual, but it's not." She looked down at the baby sucking with that oblivious need, as though she'd never tried to put it into words before. "There's this heat that spreads out and out in circles."

She said something else, but Rachel didn't catch it. She was thinking of Tony, the way he ran one finger slowly around her nipple, like he'd read about doing it in some manual, and how the pleasure it gave her was shallow, an electricity that operated only at the skin's surface.

Aja closed her eyes and sucked with a quiet but persistent smacking sound. In another minute Susan said, "She's asleep," even though she was still sucking.

When Susan had her shirt pulled down and Aja settled on her shoulder, Rachel was surprised to hear herself say, "You seem happy with her," and have it come out sounding so simple, so uncompetitive. Hadn't she always compared herself with Susan: her hair, her body, her fortune with men? Hadn't she been frustrated that her own higher grades and job achievements hadn't seemed to count in the balance, since Susan was never especially plagued by ambition? Hadn't she come that weekend to make a comparison, to use Susan's life as a measure for her own?

Now Susan was nodding, smiling at the question, running a hand over Aja's carrot-shadowed head. "And how about you?" she said, dreamy, still watching the baby. But then she snapped her head up and looked straight at Rachel. "Are you happy?"

Rachel swallowed down the rest of her coffee and signaled the waitress for a refill. Where to begin? She'd never been good at coming right out and saying what she felt; she needed to build up a picture out of the welter of details. "Things are going pretty well at work," she ventured. Though it sounded even to her own ear like an evasion, she pushed on. "They want to move me out of the Miami Beach bureau to the main city desk. The city editor told me." She took a breath. In spite of the coffee, she was determined not to sound keyed up. "It's just a matter of time. Until one of the city reporters moves somewhere."

She looked at Susan, who nodded for her to go on, and realized she hadn't been talking *to her*, she'd just been talking—as if she were across the table from almost anyone, from somebody she barely knew. And yet there had been all those years, all those small-hour sessions with their nightgowns and bottles of wine when talking to Susan had been like keeping a journal for Rachel, how she tested and searched and confirmed herself. She trained her eyes now on her friend's face, trying to feel what it meant to be saying these things to *Susan*. "I've got a really great apartment," she offered. "Sixteenth floor. Facing the ocean. You look out my living room and all you see is this incredible blue."

Susan hid a yawn behind her hand. "Sorry. It's just I've been up since five-thirty. I'm listening." She took a sip of tea. When Rachel didn't continue, she asked, "What about friends? Any people down there you're close to?"

"Some," Rachel said, and looked down at her coffee. It hadn't sounded very convincing. Susan still had it: that quiet, offhand way of zeroing in on a problem. Rachel thought of saying it would be easier when she got on the city desk, but that would come out like an excuse. She could mention Tony, but he didn't exactly qualify as a friend. This was it, what she wanted to talk about: how she felt like so much of herself was suspended, waiting for her lucky break at work or friendship or love; how she seemed still to be only paying her dues, forever paying her dues, while other people were actually living.

As she was trying to find words for this, the screen door into the bakery rattled and Hank appeared. She greeted the sight of him with a mixture of indignation and relief. She felt strangely vulnerable, precarious, as though she'd come to the brink of something and wasn't sure whether she was being held back or saved. But then she noticed something that stopped her. When Hank came around to where Susan could see him, her whole countenance fell; her grip on Aja tightened. He walked up to the table with that same bitter mouth from the airport and put his hands on the back of the third, empty chair. It was the first time Rachel had noticed his hands—how sinewy and strong they were. She realized that in the whole time she'd been with them, those hands had never once touched Susan, or Aja. Here Rachel had been thinking only of herself—her expectations, her nebulous dissatisfactions—when there was something larger, more serious, happening.

Outside, a fine drizzle was falling, and she turned her face up into it, trying to still her confusion. The rain started to come down harder as they were driving, but there was no thunder and lightning. The windshield wipers were a sobering metronome for Rachel's thoughts: *The trouble was right there from the first, and it took you this long to notice it.* Susan had dozed off by the time they got to the house. Hank nudged her, and she sleepwalked up to their room, mumbling something about waking up soon, being more lively.

Hank carried Aja into the house. He deposited her in her playpen in the living room, not carelessly but without love, the way you'd set down a grocery bag with a carton of eggs in it. He turned to Rachel, and seemed to make an effort to soften his face. "Would you mind baby-sitting awhile?"

Her first impulse was to rebel, show him she saw right through the hypocrisy of his honeyed tone. No doubt all of this, whatever it was, was his fault; her innate loyalty to Susan dictated that much. Yet there was something genuinely pleading in his eyes, something *trapped*. And maybe he felt that way: trapped by that little world of Susan and Aja, trapped by the weekend.

When he went out the door, she installed herself on the couch. Mies took up a post near the playpen, eyeing her from the floor as if she weren't entirely to be trusted. Inside the playpen Aja had a family of foam ducks, but she ignored those for a barrel-shaped plastic rattle, which she started banging over and over against the playpen floor with unvarying, monomaniacal delight, as if she were inventing noise and each new crash surprised her. Rachel left the couch and knelt at the side of the playpen. She picked up a duck and moved it as though it were swimming over a ripply surface. Aja wasn't interested. Rachel tried a different tack. She held out her hand and said, "Can I see the rattle?" in the most syrupy voice she could muster.

Aja looked puzzled for a few seconds, then took the rattle and smashed it down on Rachel's fingers. She cried out, involuntarily, and grasped the stinging hand, but Aja was already screaming her own highly articulate language of pain. Rachel froze, confused by this sudden reversal of roles that turned her into the offending party. Before she could think what to do, Mies was up and howling, Susan running downstairs. Susan scooped Aja up and started bouncing her, rubbing circles into her back. "It's all right. Mommy's here. Mommy's Aja."

Rachel squeezed her hand again, even though the smarting was just about gone. "She smashed me with the rattle," she said, and immediately felt ridiculous: a grown woman tattling on a six-month-old girl. "I just said *ow*, but it must have—"

She stopped. Susan didn't seem to be paying her any attention. The baby was quiet now, but Susan was still bouncing her, swinging her around in a circle. "Mommy's Aja. Yes."

Rachel got tired of standing there holding her hand. Did Susan make Hank feel like this—an intruder, a bungler? "Listen." She waited until Susan looked at her. "I'm going up to my room awhile."

Susan nodded. "Okay." Then she started singing "Twinkle, Twinkle." The song trailed Rachel irritatingly up the stairs to the guest room, but ended when she shut the door. She paced the old, slumping floorboards, then sat down on the futon and stared at the miniature bouquets on the wallpaper until their colors washed paler and bled. She didn't know what to think anymore, whom to be angry with. She waited, telling herself, Susan will come up, she'll come in. She remembered waiting like that in her old bedroom at home after she'd done something wrong, or when her parents had been fighting. The first and only time her father actually walked out of the house, there had been a long silence before her mother came and sat at the side of Rachel's bed. When Rachel asked her why Daddy had left, what the fight was about, her mother took her time formulating her answer, as if she were really trying to get it right, to explain. She didn't say, *Someday, when you're married, you'll understand*, though she might have. She finally took Rachel's hand and patted it. *Sometimes there just isn't air enough in a house for two people living together.* Now Rachel went to the window and looked out through the steady rain at the side yard, the gnarled figures of old apple trees, dotted with small, probably rock-hard fruit. For a person living alone there's too much air, she thought; there's only air.

She brought the second of her joints to the window and lit it, taking less care than she had the night before to shoo all the smoke out the screen, leaning her elbow into the rotting windowsill. When she'd smoked the joint almost down, she heard the front door close downstairs: Hank returning. She listened, but couldn't detect any talk. But then she did hear the two of them—it sounded like two—climbing the stairs, pausing, then walking back away, toward their bedroom. Rachel waited a few minutes, to let the smoke funnel out the window, before she opened her door. But *their* door was closed now. She approached it quietly, listened. And yes, there it was: the slow torment of bedsprings, the almost reconciled moans. Hank wouldn't be leaving. At least not now. Not this weekend.

Downstairs, Aja was asleep, cocooned in a quilt in the playpen, breathing a dream still innocent of disappointment, of loneliness. Rachel tiptoed by, as if that sleep were fragile as the union above, and went into the kitchen. She'd forgotten how heavy the pie box was, and it almost slipped from her grasp as she carried it in a precipitous arc from the fridge to the counter. She found a knife and cut a piece from the ruined part. She considered the taste of the first bite carefully. The prodigious layer of cream had actually just enough sweetness to cut the surprise of the tart, yellow heart of the pie. She consumed the second bite, and the third, more greedily, admiring the texture now, the way it dissolved in her mouth. Heavy as it was, this whipped-cream château was in the end mostly air also.

When she first heard the door and the footsteps upstairs, she froze, calculating the speed with which she could get rid of the evidence. But it was too late for that. They were already on their way down. She got a quick, improbable picture: the three of them at the table, laughing, passing around her last joint, sampling wedges of pie. She'd know right away from their faces if it was possible.

Passover Wine

I stand at least a head higher than anyone else in the synagogue, not counting my grandmother. Did that generation of
Jews just not grow any taller? Or have they all shrunk, from
age, bad digestion and the final indignity: having to spend
Sabbath morning in this low-rent excuse for a *shul* in a changing Flatbush neighborhood? I used to think of my grandmother as statuesque. She was well built and the tallest
woman in the whole family. But it's been five years since I
last came down to visit her, and she's changed. She's eighty-
two. She looks like she should be eating more. It's not that
she stoops, like some of them, but she's shorter, I'm sure of it.
I never remember my head being even with hers before.

The congregation is scattered thinly, unevenly, over the
pews. There are only a few other women. The men squint
into the prayer books, the hunched shoulders of their dark
suits draped in prayer shawls of yellowing satin. They *doven*
in jerky back-and-forth motions, muttering feverish Hebrew,
all out-of-sync. My grandmother used to *doven* and pray aloud
as fast as anyone. Today she only bends at the waist with the
movement of a tiny spasm. She mouths the prayers and nods
in time to the singing parts, but the only sound that comes
out is her difficult breath. Now and then she stops mouthing
and nodding and seems to look at a spot near the ceiling that

here is blank wall but in her old synagogue was that big stained-glass window, all dark reds and blues. I don't read the prayers. I mouth the few I'll always remember and listen to the familiar but elusive music of a language I once understood.

Some of the people whisper loudly into one another's ears. Every so often somebody notices me and my grandmother for the first time, and points at the pair of us. They also point at and talk about other people, even call out to a friend, so there's a general rumble mixed in with the prayerful muttering. When the rumble threatens to grow to a roar, the rabbi looks up from his text with a face of benign exasperation. If the *kibbitzing* doesn't stop, he says, we can't go ahead with the service.

Everything is plain about the synagogue except for the Ark. The doors are massive, sculpted gold-colored metal. The congregation comes to its feet, slowly, painfully, when the rabbi opens them. Inside are three tiers of Torahs, dressed in silver breastplates and tiny crowns polished until, even on this dim morning, they're luminous. I wonder at the fact that part of me feels strangely at rest among these old Jews, their sacred, wasted syllables eddying around me.

My grandmother grips my arm with her arthritic fingers. She leans over. It's the first thing she's said to me since we got to the synagogue: All this time you've been gone. It wouldn't have killed you to write, would it?

The service keeps on until noon. I'm starved by then. I haven't eaten a thing since a sandwich last night on the train. But before we can leave, my grandmother has to wish half the congregation good *shabbos*. You remember Mr. and Mrs. Abeles, she says. She squeezes my arm and practically pushes me into an old couple, bundled in heavy wool coats, hats and scarves, as if they don't realize it's April already. I've never

seen Mr. and Mrs. Abeles before in my life. They peer into
my face with curiosity and dawning, false recognition.

There's Rose, my grandmother says. She waves across the
synagogue. Since when is she out of the hospital?

She drags me down the aisle, elbowing her way through the
crowd, digging so hard into the flesh of my arm I'm sure she's
going to leave nail marks. So, *nu?* she says to Rose when we
reach her. They let you out? What's wrong? You forgot how
to pick up a telephone?

A light rain is falling when at last we go out. My grandmother empties her purse, but she's forgotten her kerchief. I
don't have anything I can lend her. As we walk the three
blocks to her building, slowly, arm in arm, she shivers, and the
silver bouffant of her hairdo darkens and settles over her head.
By the time we get there, her hair is totally flat. She looks into
the glass door to the lobby and runs a skittish hand over her
head. She turns to me. Her sharp features twist into a self-
mocking smile. A point of warm light flickers in her teal irises.
Maybe she has forgiven me.

My grandmother moved here from the old apartment a
couple of years ago, but the walls still look new, eggshell white.
She's taken the furniture from the old place and reupholstered
everything: ivories and pinks instead of the olives and hunter
greens, satiny cotton on what was brocade and velvet. In the
old living room the dark chairs and sofas were huddled together, but here everything is spread apart, so the space in the
middle stands out more than the furniture. From the living
room a picture window looks out over Brooklyn's low houses
and trees toward Manhattan, where on a clear day she can see
the World Trade Center. There's no sign of the porcelain
candy dish with the lid that always gave me away as a girl, if I
didn't pick it up just right.

One side wall of the living room is covered with photographs. There's the old grouping of the four grandchildren in the oval gilt frame, four small holes cut into green velvet for faces. I peer into my tiny picture. I must have been five or six, wearing a red velvet dress with a collar that's ivory in the cracking photograph. Everyone but me has sent my grandmother new pictures. She has them in Lucite box frames. My cousins look almost like strangers. There's a wedding picture of the one who's my age, and baby pictures of her little girl. I can see a trace of my cousin in the girl's face, and I study the pictures as if I might find something that has to do with me. But what I see is Frank's face yesterday morning.

I don't know what made me tell him about the abortion. He doesn't wear a look of hate. He looks at me like he doesn't know me. He tells me, I want you out of this house. I actually get down on my knees and try to take hold of his leg. He shakes me off. Get your lying Jewish ass out of here.

For lunch my grandmother has chopped herring and egg salad. I offer to help, but she says there's nothing to do. By the time she gets everything onto the table, there's a flush at her cheekbones and her forehead glistens with tiny pearls of sweat. She presses her fingers into the edge of the table and draws shallow breaths.

Take some salad. Take. She pushes the bowls in front of me. It's from Sam's on Avenue J.

I load my plate with as much as I think I can handle. She takes a spoonful of herring and tears off half a piece of rye bread. She uses the bread to push the herring onto her fork and chews with her mouth open. I always knew sooner or later you'd break it off with the *goy*, she says. Why don't you stay with Grandma awhile now?

I say I don't know. All my stuff is Upstate still.

So? You can't have it shipped down? Here at least there are Jews. Knock on wood, you could find yourself somebody.

I tell her again I don't know.

At least you had the good sense not to marry him.

There is a silence during which I think about living with Frank, waking up and making love first thing in the morning. One day we're lying there after, and he jumps out of bed. He pulls me up and says, Let's go. Let's get married. I feel good enough to almost play along, but he's serious. He'd really do it. He's actually pulling out his one suit and the tie I got him for Christmas. Sometimes when he's been inside of me, I've thought: Lovemaking like this should create something. But I know I can't marry him. Being with him is like running away, and I get homesick for parts of myself, we're so different. I tell him, Take the suit off, come back to bed. It's not even seven o'clock. We're not getting married.

I reach an arm out from under the covers, but he twists away. He stands there and glares at me. He leaves the suit pants on and steps into his boots, clomps down the bare hardwood stairs to the kitchen. In a minute I can smell his wafting cigarette.

Stay with me a couple of weeks and think it over, my grandmother says. What would be so terrible you should keep your grandmother company? And *Pesach* is coming the week after next, you know.

I must be looking back at her dumb.

Pesach. Pesach. She raises her voice and waves her arms as if I were hard of hearing. When was the last time any of you kids was here for the Seder?

She stops, and her eyes fill. What I think we both see is the table in the old apartment with all the leaves in, the starched white, the silver, the candlesticks, set for the Passover service. She wipes her eyes with the brown-spotted back of her hand and clicks her tongue on the roof of her mouth. I might not live to see another one.

We all pass our cups to my grandfather at the head of the big table when it's time to pour wine. He tilts it slowly from

the decanter, as if it were syrup. We've had only the first of
four cups and it's settled right into my knees. It's a good thing
I don't have to stand up. *Why is this night different from all
other nights?* The biggest difference is that tonight we get
drunk. Four cups. The Haggadah commands us to drink them.
God wants us to.

When we all have our cups back, my grandfather raises his.
I look around to see if I can sneak a sip, but my Aunt Rhoda
is watching me. I hold my arm up straight so it's as high as
everyone else's. The blessing, in Hebrew, then English: *King
of the Universe, who created the fruit of the vine.* Then the
wine burns thick and sweet down my throat, the whole cupful.

I slip down in my chair, ready to defend myself against anyone: tonight we're supposed to recline, to celebrate our re-
demption from bondage in Egypt. My father's tall goblet has
his name in fancy script on the side. There are cups edged
with twisted silver, black in the folds, like strands of fine rope,
and others wrapped in miniature silver grapevines. The candles throw points of light onto the metal and cut glass. From
this angle, Aunt Rhoda's breasts are enormous. If she leans
forward any more, they'll fall into her plate. My brother kicks
me under the table. What's wrong with you? he whispers into
my ear. It tickles. You never seen bosoms before? We both
start to giggle. Give me the rest of your wine, he says. He goes
for my cup.

No. I slap his hand. I finished it.

My grandfather forces a couple of coughs. My grandmother
peers at us over her reading glasses. *Vat's mit der kinder?*

After my grandfather died, my father took over running the
Seder. He and my mother ordered a new set of modern Hag-
gadahs, with watercolor pictures, from the Reform temple. My
grandmother hated it. By the time we were teenagers, the
other relatives had one by one given up making the trip to my

grandmother's Seder. It got to be just the four of us and my grandmother.

We arrive with the wine, the one thing she lets us bring. She takes the gift-wrapped bottle into the kitchen. She shrieks. What's this? Asti who? You never heard Manischewitz?

This is new, Mom, my mother says. Asti Spumante Kosher for Passover. We thought we'd try it this year. Maybe it won't be as sweet as the other.

Sweet? What, sweet? We have to drink Spanish wine at the Seder now? Jewish wine isn't good enough for you?

It's not Spanish. It's Italian, my father says.

Oh. Very fancy. And since when are the Italians such good friends to the Jews?

Such a big lawyer? You can't read? my grandmother says to my father. Everyone gets a piece of parsley to dip. Not just you.

Mother, I'm doing it this way tonight. You can all see me dipping it.

K'naka, my grandmother says. We can see. Knock on wood. We're not blind yet. What it says right here, if you want to listen a minute.

I see what it says.

Oh. Big shot. *Meshuganah*. Everything has to be a shortcut with you. If your father was alive.

Don't drag my father into this.

Steven, my mother says.

After that, my grandmother wears a martyred look for the rest of the Seder. She doesn't challenge my father, but complains and taunts him under her breath. *Mazel tov*, she says. The big expert. Knows everything. I sit at her end of the table, so woven into the Seder's shifting voices I hear the bitter countermelody.

My father reads: *When the Egyptian armies were drowning in the sea, the Heavenly Hosts broke out in songs of jubilation. God silenced them and said, My creatures are perishing and you sing praises?*

We read together: *We do not rejoice at the death of our enemy. Our triumph is diminished by the slaughter of the foe.*

Diminished, my behind, my grandmother says. You can kill the whole stinking lot of them.

My grandmother lets me help her clear the lunch table. She says she needs to lie down and rest a little bit. I ask if she'd mind my taking a walk. Mind? Why should I mind? She finds me a plastic kerchief in case the rain starts up again. She says the neighborhood isn't so good once you cross Ocean Parkway.

I pass the facades of brick row houses, blocks of two-family homes separated by the tiniest alleyways. The only touches of color are the striped plastic awnings, the rain-soaked toys on patches of yard, not yet green. I don't know how far I've walked when I feel the tearing inside. I stop on the sidewalk, one hand on somebody's fence. The sheet the doctor gave me said only moderate exercise. If I cry, I know the ripping is going to get worse. I breathe deeply. There's only one thing to do: walk back slowly and think about holding that part of me still. The tearing goes in a couple of blocks. In its place is a heat through my middle and a slow release of blood. I know it's going to be all right when I see the block with my grandmother's building.

I lie down on the couch, and when I wake up the apartment smells of roast chicken. My grandmother bends over me, puts a hand on my forehead. I tell her I'm fine. She straightens her back with a hand at the base of her spine. Come, she says. All that walking, you must be starving already.

I stand at my chair, admiring the bird's perfect, glistening skin but not hungry.

I forgot to pick up some wine like you always liked, she says. Oh, but listen what I got. She heads toward the kitchen. The Manischewitz for *Pesach*. I bought it already last week. There's always too much. She winks. You want I should open a bottle?

I tell her don't bother, I can't drink so soon after sleeping.

I'm relieved when she comes back to her seat. I couldn't stomach that sweet wine now.

But she looks disappointed. She picks up the carving set, but before she cuts she waves the fork at me. Don't say your grandmother didn't try and take care of you.

When I stayed over with my grandmother at the old apartment, she put me in the twin bed, pushed together with hers, that had been my grandfather's. His suits and bathrobe still hung in the big walnut armoire. His tortoiseshell brush and comb were poised on the mirrored dresser tray, as if someone had used them that morning. I lay there trying to see if I could still smell my grandfather, separate from the close, musty smell and the sour smell of my grandmother's breath. The sheets were always tucked in too tight.

Tonight, she wheels out a cot from the closet and sets me up in the living room. I get undressed and turn out the lights, even though I'm not sleepy. After a while, I can hear her snoring. I go to the window and quietly pull up the blind. The gray sky is suffused with the city's orange night light. At the edge of the horizon is a hazy cluster, an island of lights that must be Manhattan. I lie back on the cot and look out and pretend Brooklyn is a sea, each tiny beacon of light a boat. I run my hand up the swell of a thigh, over my belly's hollow, my breast that once more fits in a palm. My body feels like itself again. I try to and can't imagine a man making love to me. I wonder if my grandmother ever felt as if she were claiming her body back, under her nightgown inside that sheaf of a bed, after her husband died.

I can't sleep. If it's not the old apartment, it's the doctor's waiting room, or the bedroom at Frank's, the way the streetlight always shone through his thin curtain. If this keeps on I'll be up all night. Then I remember the Passover wine. I find it on a shelf in the top kitchen cabinet. I bring a glass and sit at the edge of the cot. The bottle is molded to look like a cut-glass decanter, only it has a screw top. The wine is so dark it's almost black in this light, and sweet, but not as terrible as I imagined. I think of how we dip our fingers into our cups and spill ten drops of wine, like drops of dark blood, onto our plates, for the ten plagues God visited on the Egyptians: Blood. Frogs. Lice. Wild Beasts. Blight. Boils. Hail. Locusts. Darkness. Slaying of the Firstborn.

I raise my glass. I don't have to wait for the Seder.

Dream Life

He's never paid attention to dreams the way she does. He goes to sleep and wakes up, and though he's not one of those ass-kissing, all-American, have-a-nice-day types, he gets out of bed, drops down for fifty push-ups, jumps into the shower. No, he doesn't sing. Sometimes, after his shampoo, he just stands there, right under the head, and lets the hot stream wash over him. Then he might get an intimation of something, like a cloud passing over—some dim corridor of childhood, some faceless but disturbingly familiar body in a strange bed. He shrugs his shoulders, shakes the water from his hair. He doesn't hang on to it, doesn't try to find his way back to that shadowy place, as if he might have left something he needs there.

What he needs is his towel, deodorant, a quick survey in the mirror: pectorals, biceps, cleft chin. He needs to go make coffee, but first he checks on her. She went to sleep the same time he did, maybe earlier. Since he got up she's pulled both pillows in to her chest, hooked one leg around and outside the comforter. Her face is not like the face of anyone else he's ever seen sleeping. She doesn't look lost. She looks as if she knows just where she's going, and so the lines of her mouth are sharpened by a purpose, a determination, they usually lack in her waking expression. Before he goes downstairs, he watches her for a couple of minutes, still surprised to find this woman he barely knows in his bed. And it's always with some trepidation that he climbs back up with two steaming mugs, because he's not sure he wants to hear what she's going to tell him as soon as he wakes her.

She stretches in the bed like a big, ill-tempered dog and looks at him blankly for a moment, from across a great distance. She takes a deep breath and lets out a long, throaty groan; contemplates the coffee, but doesn't sit up. And finally, what he's been dreading and waiting for: "You wouldn't believe the dream I was having."

No, he wouldn't. He's never believed it—even after two months of mornings. It isn't so much the dreams themselves, though they are certainly strange. It's that anyone could have such baroquely detailed, absolute recall; that she would recount a dream with the same urgency and conviction as a waking experience.

Maybe she was back in her eleventh-grade French class, only she couldn't speak French. She understood everything being said about Camus' *The Stranger* in an intuitive, preverbal way, but the sense of the actual words and phrases floated right past her, and she knew that if Monsieur Ricard called on her—it *was* Monsieur Ricard, and she knew that, even during the dream, only he'd taken the form of that French actor whose name she could never remember—she knew if she were called on, the game would be up. The anxiety was killingly palpable—she considered rushing the door, calculated the fall from the second-floor window—and yet at the same time, part of her was trying to talk herself out of the dream, saying she'd already graduated high school, and college, that she'd been a French Literature minor, that the people at the other desks were adults like herself, not from her high school at all but from the gym she'd recently joined, where she was the only beginner in the aerobics class.

By this time she's sitting straight-backed, cross-legged, in the middle of the bed, sucking in long drafts of coffee between run-on sentences, wincing like it's burning her throat, looking at him as though she expects a response. If he shakes his head and says, "That's wild," it sounds hopelessly insipid. If he ventures some advice—"Don't worry so much about the aerobics class. Just go and have fun"—he comes off like some watered-down pop psychologist. He never knows what to say. He always feels like he's failing her.

All of this goes, of course, for the good days, when it's only anxiety or death or the premature aging of some part of her body. She finally gets out of bed with a film of it still over her eyes, in spite of the coffee; he knows it will color her whole day, no matter how well things go, because for her the evidence of dreams is a higher authority. But it has nothing to do with *him*. He isn't the culprit. He knows that when he gets home she'll have arrived a few minutes ahead of him. She'll already have changed into jeans and a T-shirt, uncorked some red wine. Maybe she'll have picked up pâté and French bread at the market, and want to watch an old Bette Davis flic on tv. All that stays with her from the dream is an air of recollected sadness that is part of what attracts him, a vulnerability she would no doubt despise if she knew he noticed it. During a commercial, when he starts to undo her pants, she looks back at him with a solemn gratitude and he kneels in front of the couch, believing he's going to give her what he couldn't that morning.

He might not be big on champagne and roses, on soft-focus greeting cards designed for no occasion in particular except love, but he's not a bad sort. He's the kind of guy who, in the early days, liked to say that he too was a feminist; who enjoys cooking and foreign movies and music that's not rock 'n' roll. He could honestly report that since he beat up Wendy What's-Her-Name at the bus stop in fourth grade, he has never willfully abused a female, physically or emotionally. So what has he done to deserve the role he plays in her dreams?

Some mornings he arrives at the bedside with coffee, even a warm croissant—one more proof of his sensitivity, his attentions—and she greets him with a scowl. She turns away from his offerings as if he were a prison guard and she were on hunger strike. She shakes her head quickly back and forth a few times, as though when her vision cleared again she might find someone different. But here he is, and her puffy eyes narrow, sullen and hateful. "I can't believe what you were doing. I wanted to kill you."

The first few times, he tried to reason with her. How could he be held responsible—he, alive, a creature of independent volition, complete with coffee and rapidly cooling croissant—for the unconscious projections of her past frustration with men? How could she, a normally sound and rational woman, actually pin the rap of her dreams on him?

She tells him she brought him to a party at her office, and he went around talking to all of the women, casually placing a hand over one of their breasts. (He loves women's bodies, he'd be the first to admit it, but he's respectful. He'd no sooner cup his hand to a strange woman's breast at a party than he'd reach out now to touch hers, riding above the edge of the comforter, rising and falling with her indignant breath.) The women themselves did not seem to mind, or even to notice, but she couldn't take her eyes off his presumptuous hand, the way it turned his apparently sincere interest in the conversation into vile condescension, hypocrisy.

While she relates all this, he has the peculiar sensation of a man falsely accused of a crime, but with no verifiable alibi. If he lets himself take it too seriously, the sensation assumes a nightmarish quality, the kind of double-reality anxiety *she* feels in her impossible classrooms. He tries to make light of it, to sympathize: "That's really crazy. I would have been furious too." But she won't let him partake of her outrage. That would constitute dangerous fraternization. She glares at him even more fiercely. Then he gets angry himself. "This is ridiculous. Why don't you skip your aerobics class and go see a therapist?" But of course, that approach is suicide—showing himself to be just the kind of loutish, insensitive boor who would do precisely what he did (but he didn't do it; it wasn't he!) at the party.

At a loss for other strategies, he sits at the side of the bed—innocent, aggrieved. He says very quietly that the coffee is going to get cold. He mentions offhandedly that the new Godard film opened last night at the Nickelodeon, and she glances at him suspiciously, like a child who wants to stay mad but can feel herself softening. If he treads lightly like this, goes back downstairs without a word, having finished the croissant himself but leaving her coffee, she might appear at the kitchen door, in his bathrobe. "So you'd never do anything like that?"

He shakes his head, doing his best not to look impatient, ironical.

She takes a couple of tentative steps into the room. "It's just that while it's happening, it feels so *real*."

Looking back, he can't exactly locate the change, but at some point the bad-guy dreams begin to affect him. Each morning he brings the coffee up more and more sheepishly. Maybe there's something to the dreams after all; maybe they reflect a darker side of his character she intuitively perceives, that he's always been loath to acknowledge. Now he sips his coffee at the side of the bed before waking her, prolonging the reprieve of his ignorance, all the while knowing it has to end, like a drunk who's waiting to hear what he did last night during his blackout. It's as if he's taken on this other, double life that only she can reveal to him.

Sometimes he's turned a petty discussion into a major argument, out of a wild, senseless petulance; once he brought another woman home, and expected *her* to sleep on the sofa bed; a couple of times he slapped her around. When she tells him, he doesn't protest. He can't bring himself to actually apologize, but he bows his head; he's ashamed to look at her. Sometimes he takes the rest of his coffee down to the kitchen. He can understand that she'd want to be alone. After ten or fifteen minutes, she might come down to make toast, but they'll hardly speak. On his way out he'll give her one long look, beseeching and penitent. He'll reach out as if to touch her, then let his arm drop.

It's around this time that they stop making love. He doesn't want her any less than he used to, but he feels unworthy. He sits next to her at the movies, his hand in the dark air over her thigh, wavering like a teenager's. He eyes her across the front seat on the drive home, hoping she might slide closer. She isn't unfriendly toward him. In fact, it seems to take her less time now to snap out of the bad-guy-dream spell, as if his guilt were displacing her anger. She isn't unfriendly, only completely asexual. And he knows it's only right that she make the first move.

A month ago, he would have given anything to stop her daily reports on her dreams. But now, after three or four mornings like this, he wouldn't even mind being the bad guy. At least then it was *him*, some extension, however perverse, of *their* relationship. At least then, if someone had to play the role of her archetypal male, it was *he* playing it. Now that she's stopped recounting her nightly adventures, he can't help feeling he's been replaced—and not by some other bad guy. This morning he wakes up early and watches her. Sure enough, her expression is different: not even the usual abandon of sleep, but a specific abandon.

A smile spreads slowly over her face, the same smile she used to get at the start when he touched her. Her breathing changes and she shifts positions, pushes off the comforter. The strong curve of her back is turned toward him and he can see, outlined under the sheet, her left leg, bent out like a wing. Then in one sharp movement, she shifts again to face him, curled inward, knees tight together. That's when it happens: the few crazy breaths and the shudder down her whole body.

What he wants to do is tiptoe around the bed, slip in behind her, touch her until she shudders like that again; wakes up shuddering and realizes it was he, it has always been he. But it's too late already. She's stirring, feeling for the comforter, pulling it over her breasts. In another minute her eyes are open. For that first, unguarded instant, she looks disappointed to see him, then guilty. But then she collects herself enough to get annoyed, as if he'd walked in on some private activity. "Now you're watching me sleep?"

He doesn't even care that she's angry. He feels well within his rights. But he gets up and leaves the room, anyway, because he's afraid otherwise he'll grab her by the shoulders, shake her and start shouting, "Who is he?"

Talk to yourself just as you're falling asleep. Tell yourself, "I'm going to remember everything." That's what she suggested in the beginning, when he first confessed he never remembered his dreams. Now he's tried it for three nights in a row, and nothing has happened. His mornings are no different, except that he doesn't have *her* dreams, or even her, to contend with. It isn't so much that he misses her, this new loneliness. It's that he's begun to suspect he's missing something inside himself; that, by virtue of an unjustly defective or barren subconscious, he's been excluded from this whole other side of life that's so rich for her.

Tonight he spends a long time making dinner, reads every magazine in the house. When he finally gets into bed, he refuses to talk to himself about dreams; he doesn't want to set himself up for one more disappointment. Sometime in the middle of the night, the phone rings—seven, eight times. It doesn't wake him, but it enters his sleep, distinctly enough for him to think that it's probably she who's calling; that she must have awakened out of some dream. Maybe she dreamed they were together again, and it was so good, she understood that she'd made a mistake. "It's all my fault," she would say if he answered. "It was just those stupid dreams that messed everything up." Even though it's two A.M., she'd insist on coming right over.

The hand that slips under the comforter is like cool silk, and he knows right away it is hers. She whispers his name again and again, until the breathy syllables seem to surround him. Before he can say a word, she's on top of him, arching back, perfect, almost untouchable in the aura of streetlight. He places a hand on each of her breasts to guide her, and she throws her head back and laughs, until the sounds change to an even wilder music.

He sits up with a start. His chest is slippery with sweat. The room is absolutely still, but his ears are ringing, the way the air seems to be shimmering long after an orchestra has played the last note. He should get up and rinse himself off. But maybe he'll call her back first.

Pressure
for Pressure

The girl must have been nervous, flipping through *People* magazine so fast she couldn't be seeing anything, cracking her gum with a sideways snap of the jaw—the same way Anna herself had done when she was a teenager, but more exaggerated, desperate, so that each time her mouth pulled away from itself it looked to Anna like the girl was practically wincing. Anna turned away from her, back to the novel that sat unopened in her own lap. She was trying to find and hold on to a center of calm she'd had when she woke that morning but that had slipped away from her in the clinic waiting room. The place was cheerful enough, but everything in it seemed treacherous with significance: the wall mural of women holding hands, like a string of paper cut-out dolls; the receptionist at the front desk, who'd looked up at Anna from the appointment book with an expression of studied neutrality, almost but not quite as if Anna were only here for a checkup; the big bay window, sharp with a tauntingly ordinary July morning sun. And worst of all, the girl, sitting across a coffee table adorned with not one but three copies of *Our Bodies, Ourselves*.

She couldn't have been more than eighteen or nineteen. She was pretty in a young sort of way, in spite of how she ringed her pale eyes with dark purple liner. There was an uneasy, transparent defiance about her skin-tight black jeans, her almost-flat chest beneath the white muscle T-shirt that read, *Fool for love* in black script. Anna herself had on an old India-print dress she usually wore only at home these days, that hung in such loose folds her body was unrecognizable.

The chime on the entry door rang, and a pregnant woman wearing a baby blue sweat suit walked in, her belly riding high and far out in front of her. The receptionist smiled. "How are you feeling today?"

The woman ran a hand over her swollen middle, as if she were checking. Anna shot a quick glance at the girl, who had stood up, her hands pressed down in what looked like fists in her pockets. Only when the pregnant woman had gotten her prescription and left did the girl sit back down. Anna wanted to tell her to relax. You didn't associate a pregnancy like that, a real pregnancy, with what Anna was here for, what the girl was no doubt here for too. Anna knew that much from her first time, or thought she knew. Because now as she looked at the girl staring into her lap, she thought of that perfect, ripe belly and felt something turning inside her, something sour and suspiciously like regret. She took a deep breath and let it out slowly. It was only the girl who was setting her off like this. All she needed to keep her cool was to mind her own business.

In another couple of minutes, the receptionist came around into the waiting area. She wore a pair of those wide, squared-off Earth sandals whose basic principle of comfort seems to be letting feet *spread*, and her legs were woolly with long, golden hair. Anna suddenly wished she could cover up her own calves, the hard black stubble just starting back like some unkillable weed. In the crook of her arm the receptionist cradled two clipboards. "Sorry to keep you so long," she said. "We were waiting for another patient, but she doesn't seem to be coming." She held the clipboards out, one to Anna, one to the girl. "Why don't you fill out these forms, and we'll get you two started."

There was something about the way the woman said *you two*, as if Anna and the girl were together, that made Anna meet the girl's gaze, squarely, for the first time. A veil seemed to fall away from the girl's face in that moment. She looked even younger—scared, but more than that, beseeching, as if she wanted or expected something from Anna. Anna looked away, picked up the pen chained to the top of the clipboard and turned to the first form. NAME. DATE. DATE OF LAST PE-RIOD. PREVIOUS PREGNANCIES. METHOD OF BIRTH CONTROL USED. She was ashamed to write simply "none," as if she herself were some ignorant teenager. Instead she wrote "diaphragm/rhythm." It had always worked for her, ever since that "previ-ous pregnancy" nine years earlier, when she discovered her body did in fact work the way the textbooks said it would. She used the diaphragm most of the month, but cut herself a few days' slack on either end of her period. When this last pe-riod hadn't come, her reaction had been first disbelief, later anger. She couldn't help feeling double-crossed by her body, as if it had begun encroaching on even her small margin of free-dom for its own ends.

Anna worked the lunch shift at the restaurant with a woman named Leslie, a single mother with a two-year-old girl. Anna liked to ask Leslie questions, feeling a little like a curious child herself, a kid sister. Leslie was twenty-nine, just a year older than Anna, but she seemed to Anna to be a grown woman, while Anna herself didn't feel like one. Just that spring, they were in the back room, wiping down silverware with old cloth napkins soaked in club soda. Anna was asking Leslie whether she'd actively wanted a child, or just fallen into it. Leslie stopped wiping, and her spoon caught the light of the small, open window. "For a year or two I had this feel-ing. Every month," she said. "When I'd ovulate. It's hard to explain, but it was like this hum." Leslie stared at the spoon for a moment, as if she were remembering something beauti-ful beyond words.

Anna had never felt anything like that. She smiled bitterly to herself as she filled out DATE OF LAST PERIOD on the third, pastel form. Her ovaries didn't announce themselves as they yearned toward their destiny. They were furtive. They slunk, they sneaked up on her.

When Anna had finished her forms the girl was still busy writing. She hunched her long torso over the clipboard and her face was screwed up with effort, as though she were at school taking a test in her most difficult subject. Anna looked out the bay window, and wondered about the woman who hadn't shown up. Had she miraculously gotten her period at the last minute? Or had she changed her mind, decided to go through with the pregnancy? Maybe she'd made up her mind on her own. Or maybe she had a husband or boyfriend who'd talked her into it. Anna didn't have to worry about that. She had a boyfriend, more or less. The way she preferred to put it was that she was *seeing somebody*. But he didn't know about this.

She'd met Tom at the restaurant—one of the local business people who came in fairly often for lunch—but ironically, the restaurant was what helped her keep him at a comfortable distance. In the beginning, he used to show up at the bar toward the end of her dinner shift. After a few times, she'd asked him to stop. She said she liked to have a drink or two after work with the other waiters and waitresses, then go home to bed. "I'm too tired to enjoy you," she'd said, smiling a coy, suggestive smile that she hoped would make him feel good. She liked to see a man a couple of times a week. That way you got close enough to be able to talk and have decent sex, but not so close the guy started to think he had to move in with you. Given the pattern she'd established with Tom, it wouldn't be so hard to get through the next two weeks, when she wasn't supposed to have intercourse. The first week she planned on faking a summer flu; the second, an out-of-town visitor. She'd figured it would help if she talked to him a lot on the phone, even sent some sweet card to say how much she missed him.

When the receptionist came back for the clipboards, the girl shot Anna the kind of helpless, sinking look she remembered from high school, the kind the slower students wore when the tests got turned in. The woman motioned for them to follow, and Anna let the girl walk out first, down the hallway into a small room with charts and plastic models of the female anatomy. "Take a seat," the woman said, pointing to a line of three old wicker chairs, no doubt part of the clinic's efforts to keep the place homey. "Sherry will be your counselor today. She'll be with you in a few minutes to explain the procedure."

As soon as the woman left, the girl jumped up from her seat. "I figured you were having one too. I'm Gag," she said.

Anna gave her a funny look, partly because of the name itself, partly because of the urgency with which she presented it.

"I mean, my real name is Margaret."

The girl shrugged and went pink at the cheekbones, as if even she knew the nickname was silly, just an attempt to sound tough, and Anna couldn't help smiling. "I'm Anna," she told her.

She hoped they'd get through the formalities and then just sit and wait, but the girl paced a few times and turned on her. "You done this before?"

Anna nodded, then immediately regretted admitting it. She got a picture of that other waiting room, her first time, of the dozen women seated in a circle for a lecture on birth control, and she saw herself as she must have looked then, at nineteen, a college kid shipped across town to the city hospital, her only thought wanting to get the thing over with, to slide back into her life. There had been a skinny Chinese girl who'd started crying when the lecture turned to the subject of rubbers and foam, and hadn't been able to stop. And then there was the barrel-shaped black woman who stood and faced the group when the nurse called her name. "Don't let them tell you it don't hurt," she bellowed, yanking her arm out of the anxious grasp of the nurse. "I've had five children and two of these, and it hurts like the devil. They lying if they tell you different."

Anna could still see her face as the nurse dragged her off, looking back at the circle of women who at least for that afternoon were her sisters in the shame Anna hadn't yet understood: an angry, startled look, as though her whole life was a subject about which she'd been misled.

"It's not so bad," Anna said, as much to herself as the girl.

The girl considered this, making quick work of the nails on one hand—not biting them, only running her bottom teeth behind each one as if she were cleaning them. "My friend Debbie—her sister. She had one."

Anna waited to hear what the sister had said, but the girl only turned and stared for a moment at the anatomy poster. Then she spun around with a new question: "You married?"

Anna shook her head, wondering just how old and shapeless she looked to the girl in her Indian dress.

"You got a boyfriend, then?"

Anna said, "Not really." She wasn't sure why she lied, or if she really was lying. She had a vision of Tom making coffee the morning before, in her bathrobe—floor-length on Anna, but barely covering his knees. "How about you? You have somebody?"

"I thought I did." The girl sat down at the edge of the wicker chair nearest Anna. "Son of a bitch." She didn't say anything for a minute, and when she did, her voice sounded different, quieter but somehow tighter, too. "When I told him, he got scared. He didn't want to have anything to do with me. His best friend had to lend me the money. You believe that?" She pushed her unruly hair back off her forehead, and for a second Anna could picture her in one of the high ponytails she herself had worn when she was younger. "I saw him at the bar last night, and you know what? I threw a drink in his face." She looked at Anna, brazen and sheepish at the same time.

"At least you found out," Anna said. "He was like that."

"Yeah, sure." The girl took a dig at one thumbnail and tossed her head back. "Aren't most of them?"

"No," Anna said. Then she amended it: "I don't know."

The girl sank, deflated, into the back of her chair, as though she'd expected some wisdom Anna obviously didn't possess. She started pulling a piece from a nail that was already so short, Anna was sure she was going to draw blood. Part of Anna wanted to lean forward, put a hand on her shoulder, her knee. And yet the girl might easily have flinched, pushed her hand off. Anna still hadn't moved when the door opened and a short, suntanned woman walked in. Her smiled seemed well practiced but genuine.

"I'm Sherry," the woman said. She looked about Anna's age; looked, with her hiking shorts and tank top and running shoes, like the kind of woman Anna might have been friendly with. She sat in the chair that faced Anna and the girl, and slapped her hands down on her knees. "Everyone ready?"

"I was ready an hour ago," the girl said, under her breath but loud enough. "When I got here."

Anna shot the girl a hard look. But Sherry wasn't thrown; her face immediately arranged itself into a picture of patience. "We're going to get you moving as quickly as we can," she said. "What I want to do now is run through the procedure, step by step."

Anna nodded to Sherry—professional, woman-to-woman— in hopes of setting herself apart from the girl, hunched in her seat with a face of sullen mistrust. Anna tried to fix the girl with a serious eye, as if to say, *Listen*, but she was already studying her fingernails, planning her next attack.

Nobody had bothered, Anna's first time, to explain much,

except how to avoid landing back there for another go-round. And the procedure itself had been different. Anna forced herself to focus on Sherry, who was holding up a thin plastic tube which Anna imagined moving up inside her toward that tiny inner opening. This time there would be only the one, slender piece, with the suction apparatus—also plastic—attached to the end of it. Not that series of ever-larger metal pipes threading the eye of the speculum and that inner eye—how many of them had there been? Not that squat, green-steel oil furnace of a machine droning on beyond her feet in the stirrups, beyond the bald head of the doctor who kept saying, "That a girl. We're going to scrape it all clean."

Anna missed the rest of what Sherry was saying. She was remembering the Vaseline-focus poster taped to the ceiling above where she lay, a chestnut mare and her foal in a field of spring grass. Remembering how she'd tried to keep her eyes on the picture, to travel out of her body to that lush pasture where she was more child than mother. But when it was over, when her body cramped around the space left as the metal slipped out of her, she'd turned from the picture too soon, in time to see the nurse's hand, the murky vial of blood she carried from the machine to the trash can.

"Are you all right?" Sherry was leaning toward her as if something had happened, and Anna did in fact feel like she had come out of a swoon.

The girl was looking at her too, with a cross between concern and a grim fascination. "All right?" the girl said. "She's green."

Anna smiled to reassure them. "I'm fine. Go on. I'm sorry." She smoothed her dress over her legs. "I was just remembering something."

"No second thoughts?" Sherry's face wore an expression Anna might expect from a shrink's—a kindness that seemed to want to draw her over some precipice. "Because you've still got some time to think this thing through."

"I've thought it through." She felt a catch of irritation in her voice the woman didn't deserve. But really, she'd never figured there was much to think about. You couldn't spend the night with a baby, then send it away for a couple of days while you got back a sense of *your space*; you couldn't count on those fragile equations of obligation and need she so scrupulously balanced in her adult relationships.

By the time Sherry measured their blood pressure, Anna felt only the slightest bit shaky. Sherry said the final thing she needed was blood samples. The girl looked right at her arm as the needle entered it, even kept her eyes on the rising column of red. Anna willingly held out her arm but turned to the wall, the anatomy poster.

When Sherry left the room with the samples, the girl stood and faced Anna, her thumbs slung in her belt loops. "You looked like you were going to pass for a minute there." She pulled out one side of her mouth, though she didn't have any more gum. "You're the one who's supposed to be Miss Experience."

"Let's drop it if you don't mind."

"Hey, okay." The girl made an I-don't-care face, flashed her two outspread palms in a gesture of noninterference. "Excuse me. I just thought you might want to talk, that's all."

Anna said, "I don't want to talk," and was surprised by the vehemence of her tone.

The girl looked taken aback, but quickly pulled herself up. "Fuck you," she said. "What's your problem?"

"Look. Gag, Margaret. I'm sorry."

"Right," she said, and sat back down in the seat one over from Anna's. "Don't worry about it." She pulled her T-shirt down from her sides, so the letters of *Fool for love* stretched, momentarily distorted, over her chest. "I'm just going to sit here and think about bacon and eggs."

When Sherry opened the door, Anna and the girl had been sitting for a couple of minutes in an uneasy silence. Sherry

said "Margaret," and the girl was up on her feet. Anna thought
she was going to follow Sherry out without even looking back;
but she did, for an instant, before the door closed. Her makeup
had spread a little; inside the humid purple rings her eyes
burned, and her mouth had a hard, almost superior set to it.

Once the girl was gone, Anna went to the room's one small
window, facing out back toward the parking lot, ringed with an
encroaching border of weeds. The window was stuck, painted
shut, but she banged and heaved until she managed to lift it.
The sun had already risen high enough to beat down on the
lot, and the smell that came in on the whisper of breeze was a
mixture of something sweet from the weeds and hot asphalt
that turned Anna's stomach. She'd felt the nausea already a few
times at the restaurant, looking at food that usually tempted
her, walking into the bar's atmosphere of liquor and smoke. It
had never gotten particularly bad—just enough to keep her
from forgetting her body wasn't itself.

Anna left the window and sat back down. Her eyes traveled
again to the anatomy poster, the definite bulge of the belly in
profile—a graphic trick to accommodate all the organs. Anna's
own belly was bloated. She put her hand over it, plump and
round like a Buddha's under the Indian dress. Her breasts too
were noticeably fuller, and *tight*, as if pressing out against the
confining shape of her skin. For a moment Anna tried to imagine giving up, giving in to the fullness, letting her body go its
own way. She tried to imagine Tom's face when she told him.
She thought of Tom at the picnic they'd had a few weeks before with Leslie and Leslie's little girl, Rose. While Anna and
Leslie laid out the blanket and put together the sandwiches,
Tom taught Rose "Twinkle, Twinkle," all the way through,
repeating the verses over and over in a patient litany to the
girl on his lap.

Anna was still a week away from her period, she had no
cause to suspect, and so she'd seen Tom's attentions to Rose
as a lark, a favor to Leslie. It was only now, in reviewing the

picture, that she read a deeper longing into his persistence. It wasn't so much a longing for fatherhood; Tom had never struck her as a guy who was wild about kids. It was more a desire to get close. Anna called up the scene again, and remembered how Tom kept looking back at her from his corner with Rose, as if he wanted to make sure she took notice, as if it were his way of showing her he could be that gentle. And after all, wasn't that the reason Anna hadn't told him she was pregnant? Not that he'd have some asshole response like Gag's teenager; not that he'd feel one way or another about having a child, or not having one. Simply that he'd want to comfort her, to be part of what she went through, and so become more a part of her.

Anna wasn't wearing her watch, but it seemed ten minutes had surely gone by since Sherry had taken the girl. It couldn't be long now before Anna's turn. She felt herself trembling a little, in spite of the heat. To calm herself, she made a quick calculation: in an hour or so, she'd be out of there. When she was finished the time at the hospital, her roommate, Joan, had been waiting, with her enormous, toothy smile and an outstretched cigarette. Joan had been all ready to take Anna back to the dorm and put her to bed. She'd even gotten a bunch of daffodils for Anna's nightstand. She couldn't believe it when Anna told her to pull in at the diner on the road back to school, and when she ordered a double cheeseburger, fries. Even Anna herself had been surprised at her appetite. She finished everything and then ordered ice cream, too, overruling Joan's advice about taking it easy. It was as though she were eating to forget, or to fill something.

She had no appetite now, even though she'd followed the rules, and hadn't touched any food or drink since just before bedtime. But she did need some coffee. She could feel the headache just starting, reaching out like the fingers of a hand over the top of her skull. She let her head drop down and pressed her thumbs into the spots at her temples. She held them there for a minute with her eyes closed, trying to feel her energy moving away from the headache, out of her head and down into her body. She was sitting like that when Sherry knocked once on the door and then opened it. Anna rose and stepped forward. She took a deep breath and gave a grim little smile to Sherry, who smiled back the perfect, protocol smile: all comfort, with no trace of joy.

The room where the procedure took place had one poster on the wall but none on the ceiling. Sherry left her there, with a white paper hospital gown, to undress. The room was on the side of the building away from the sun, and Anna broke out in goose bumps when she took off her dress. A chill ran up her back, where the gown hung open, and the woman doctor who knocked and came in noticed right off she was shivering. "Have a seat on the table, Anna," the doctor said.

She was an older woman, probably in her fifties. Her short, straight hair had mostly gone gray, and there was a maternal effectiveness about the way she produced a yellow blanket out of a cabinet, opened the blanket and had it around Anna's shoulders in one single motion. Anna never got to look very closely at her face. Before she knew it, she was leaning back on the padded table, lifting her knees into a set of stirrups—molded plastic, so they were cool but not cold. "Come down a little more," the doctor said. "Good." Out of the corner of her eye, Anna could see the doctor, her hands slipping easily into a pair of surgical gloves. "Now I'm going to get you ready for the speculum."

In spite of the doctor's announcement, Anna felt herself tense up at the first touch. But the doctor had jelly on the finger that just quickly probed her. "Now I'm going to put in the speculum"—plastic too, and in very quickly, clicked open with just a small shudder. When Anna looked past the blanket, past her own knees, she saw the doctor's hands again, and the needle. She stopped listening and shut her eyes, took a few long breaths and one short gasp when the shot came.

"Now I'll be inserting the tube." Anna's eyes were back open, but she didn't look down to see it. She could picture the tube in her mind, the one Sherry had shown them. She kept her eyes on the ceiling, kept breathing, and it was in, jiggling around while the doctor got some kind of clamp on it. And there it was: that ache on the cervix that wasn't quite pain, that didn't feel like pain anywhere else on the body. She heard the receptionist on the phone the week before when she'd made the appointment: "You're free to bring a partner into the procedure room with you"—as if she were going to give birth. She got a picture of the skinny old black nurse who'd stood tableside and held her hand the first time—how frail she looked, but what strength in those fingers, so though Anna clutched that hand until she was sure the nurse would cry out, the woman had matched her, pressure for pressure.

The clamp was on, and the suction unit must have gotten hooked onto the tube. The doctor didn't say anything this time, but just started working. Much as she tried to keep it steady, Anna felt her breath coming in and out in quick spasms. It was as if someone were pulling at her insides with sharp little tugs. She grasped the sides of the table, which were metal. What would it have been like to have Tom there, to have been gripping his hand? After an instant's release, the pulling started again, more violent this time. "Almost finished now."

There were just a few more tugs, and then the doctor was unclamping the instruments and slipping them out of her, easing her knees down from the heights of the stirrups, pulling the blanket down over her legs. She wasn't sure why she started to cry, except that she could, it was over, and she remembered from the other time, too, how small you felt after, how fragile.

The doctor had left. Someone knocked and came in. It was Sherry. Anna wished it were someone else, but she let the woman take her hand anyway, and was surprised to find herself squeezing it hard. Why was it that even though she'd never dreamed of wanting a baby, she had this sudden, crazy feeling of loss?

"It's okay." Sherry used her other hand to smooth the blanket across Anna's shoulder. "You're all done now."

Anna fitted the sanitary minipad Sherry gave her inside her underpants, and carefully slipped them on. She followed Sherry down the hall with stiff little steps, her feet spread wide, as though she were carrying something large and breakable between her legs.

Sherry set down Anna's clothes on a bench inside the door to the recovery room. There were six beds, all empty except for the one with the girl. When Anna and Sherry came in, she propped herself up on her elbow. "Can I get dressed now?"

The girl looked pale to Anna, and Sherry must have thought so too. "Why don't you wait another few minutes," she told her.

Sherry led Anna to a bed one removed from the girl's. Anna wanted to curl up on her side. She didn't want to face the girl, but she couldn't just turn her back on her. When Sherry left, the girl sat all the way up in bed. "So. That's it," she said.

Anna gave a weak nod.

"You were right," the girl said.

Just then Anna got a wild cramp. She tried to focus on the girl, as if that might help her.

"About it not being so bad."

Anna meant to say "Yeah," but the word sounded only inside her head. She looked away from the girl, turning her eyes close in to where she was hugging herself under the blanket. She thought surely the girl would realize she didn't want conversation, but she kept on. "They better let me out of here soon. My friend's been waiting out there half an hour already. It's going to kill her whole lunch break."

Anna's cramps were coming harder now, and there was that

kink in her cervix as though the tube were still there. But it didn't seem to matter to the girl that Anna was barely listening.

"You know that guy I told you about? As soon as they let me out of here, I'm going to look for him. I bet I know where he'll be, too." Her eyes flashed, triumphant. "At Ranger's. Playing pinball. Bet anything." She threw back the sheet that was covering her legs, long and skinny—a girl's legs still, not a woman's. She turned away from Anna to pull on her jeans. They were tight enough that Anna could make out the line of the sanitary pad under them. "I'd like to see what he has to say to me now."

Anna closed her eyes, and was only dimly aware of the girl as she finished dressing, of Sherry, who came in to say that yes, she could go. The cramps were still coming, but easier. Anna felt the sun from the window on her hair, on her eyelids. She imagined she was under the quilt in Tom's bed, where the sun came in like this first thing in the morning.

She woke at the small disturbance of Sherry taking a seat at the side of the bed. She stretched out her legs and realized she felt almost nothing through her middle. "It's been more than an hour," Sherry said. "You'll probably want to be getting dressed now."

Anna stretched again, but kept lying there. She didn't want to get up. She would have liked to turn over, keep sleeping. But Sherry stood and brought to the bed the little pile Anna had made of her dress and her espadrilles. "You'll feel better once you're up and moving around," she said.

Anna sat up in the bed to reassure Sherry, but waited until she was alone to do anything more. Even though nothing hurt, she moved slowly. When she was dressed, she looked around the room, as if there might be something she was forgetting. She straightened the blanket and sheet, even though she knew the beds were probably stripped after every patient. She drew her dress up in folds and slipped down her underpants to check the napkin, but it was perfectly clean. Over the coming days, though, there would be something. Not blood exactly, something blacker: the last, dead bits of lining. She wondered if the girl would know that was all it was, if the dark tissue would frighten her.

Anna was ready, but she didn't leave the room until Sherry came back for her. Sherry was holding a small bottle of apple juice, and Anna accepted it. She took a couple of tiny sips, then a longer one. She was drinking when Sherry asked her: "Is somebody going to come for you?"

Anna had planned this out in advance: how she'd say she had a friend with an office on the next block; how she'd just be driving that far, and then her friend would take over. But now, looking at this woman who, after all, had taken her hand, she couldn't go through with it. "No. I mean, I'm not sure."

Sherry gave her an unruffled, appraising look. "Would you like to use our phone?" she said.

The telephone was behind the front desk. The receptionist was gone, and Sherry left her, so there was no one within earshot but a little girl in the waiting room. The first time she rang Tom's office, she greeted the busy signal with relief. She realized she had no idea what to say if he answered. She waited a minute, watching the little girl on the floor, whispering some secret into the ear of a ragged stuffed Snoopy. When she picked up the phone to dial again, she still didn't know, but she wasn't sorry to hear the sharp ring, then the silence, like a holding of breath. Someone would answer, probably Tom. And whether it was the right thing or not, she would say something.

Life Drawing

The two-minute poses: She stretches her arms overhead ballet-style. She bends at the waist and sweeps a hand toward the floor. She turns sideways to the class and arches her back, lifts her chin to the ceiling; her arms fall behind her like wings. The hurried scratching of charcoal doesn't cover her heartbeat.

The half-hour poses: She sits down on the quilt, hugs her knees to her chest and stares into an abstract landscape on the gallery wall, the white space around it. She thinks about a movie she's seen, *The Year of Living Dangerously*. The man who was also alone at the theater, who probably noticed her. She thinks a kind of excited emptiness. The stiffness steals down into her hips. One whole side from the waist down is asleep. For the last five minutes she concentrates on not changing her facial expression.

The last, longest pose: She curls up in fetal position, drifts off. Someone says, "It's nine o'clock," and she wakes, she unfolds her body. The students compare drawings, pack up their charcoals and pads, their lapboards or easels. She goes to the washroom to dress and puts the check in her pocket. Filling her head is a deep buzzing that stays with her out into the night.

She had no idea who he was when he called. There was a silence after his name, until he said, "From the life drawing class." Then she got the picture of a small man with wire-rimmed glasses who sat on the left side of the circle. He cleared his throat. He was wondering if she was available for modeling jobs outside the gallery. He needed someone.

When she left for his place, the sun was going down, and she could feel a chill coming. She was glad she'd brought a robe and warm socks for in between poses. She couldn't help thinking she must be naive. Taking her clothes off at the gallery was fine. Impersonal. But at his house? She could turn around and call him from the gas station a few miles back, tell him she couldn't make it. But this was a modeling job. Twenty dollars plus gas money. It was sheer vanity to imagine the man had anything else on his mind.

It was dusk when she got to the farmhouse. Woodsmoke snaked reassuringly from the chimney. She took her bag and shut the car door. When he let her in, she was friendly. "Not at all. The drive was beautiful."

She surveyed the interior of the house. He must have re-modeled the place, taken down a few walls. It was all like one big room around the brick chimney. There was a narrow staircase, almost a ladder, that probably led up to the bedroom. The walls were hung sparingly with paintings and drawings she figured were his.

He was about her height when she took off her clogs. If she went past his glasses, he really wasn't bad-looking. He had a serious face and fine hands. Funny, she'd never taken much notice of him at the gallery.

"Nice place," she said.

He said thanks and offered her something to drink.

She said, "No, that's okay. But I really could use your bathroom."

He pointed across the living room toward a door that hung partway open.

"I guess I may as well change now, too," she said.

She shut the door behind her. The bathroom was small and

clean. On the wall was one gorgeous black-and-white photograph of a nude underwater. She looked in the mirror, then took off her clothes. It was cold, standing there, but she took a minute to study herself. In the mirror she could see her body from the waist up. She tightened her stomach. She twisted to look at her arched lower back and the profile of her breast, the peak of a nipple that was hard in this air. She put on her robe, made a neat pile of her clothes and went back to him.

He wanted to begin with the short poses, the way they did at the gallery. For the first time she had trouble coming up with different positions, felt uncertain when she struck a pose. She was really no ballerina. But he said, "Good," or "Perfect. Hold it right there."

He was moving his charcoal over the pad at a feverish pace, and she started to wonder what was appearing there. She chose a simple position, facing him, one foot resting on the other knee. What she saw on the paper was nothing like what she'd expected: not a body but a series of forms, metamorphosing one into another, abstract but suggestive. She could imagine one as an inner thigh, one as the hill of a buttock, and the dark, cross-hatched joints where the forms began or ended or folded together as crevices, secret vaginas.

His eyes shot up and down between her and the pad. The way his glasses reflected the studio light, it was hard to tell what part of her body he was looking at. She started watching his hands, moving over the paper like intelligent animals.

She hadn't changed poses for maybe five minutes. The knee of her standing leg might never move again, and she laughed and hobbled in a small circle. He smiled, but she thought that behind his glasses his eyes were still serious. He said, "I really like drawing you."

She looked up and felt her cheeks flush. He asked her if she got high. She said yes. He said how about smoking a joint and then doing a long pose. She considered putting on her robe while he got the joint from a box and hunted for matches. But it was warm by the wood stove, and such an act of modesty was pointless now.

He handed her the lit joint. She looked down at her chest that swelled as she took in the smoke, that sweet, tingling helplessness all through her body. Now that he was no longer drawing, he looked only at her face. It made her feel strange, as if her naked body were an outfit all wrong for the occasion.

He set her up for the pose on his big drafting table: on her side facing him, legs pressed together, her head resting on her outstretched arm. The way she was turned, she was looking right at him. She tried to focus on some object in the room and move into the kind of reverie she had at the gallery. But she was curious.

There was a form taking shape on the paper, but it was a minute before she could see that it was her shoulder. He drew slowly now. He studied her shoulder carefully, considered it, even as he rubbed charcoal on paper. Did his concentration have anything to do with the fact that her shoulder was lovely? When he looked at it, delicately rendered it, was he thinking of her? He moved from her shoulder up to the curve of her neck. He tilted his head onto the plane of her head to look at it, to trace the line of her collarbone with the charcoal wand in midair, as if stroking her.

From the collarbone he moved down to the tight arc of her breast. She may have colored some under the spotlight, but he didn't notice anything. He was drawing her breast on the paper. He didn't just make a line but conjured the shape from shadings and gentle smudges of charcoal, so it came to life little by little as she watched. She could recognize it as her breast but also as something apart, as beautiful. It was like watching a mirror that made her image visible only gradually in a very favorable light, at once confirming and creating her.

He bent down close over the pad. When he straightened, she could see that he'd drawn the nipple so that it was dark and firm. The breast seemed to hover in the air of the page, like a fantasy, like desire.

What would he say if she asked for the picture? He was looking full at her now. The side she was leaning on was pins and needles.

Madame Bartova's School of Ballet

The first time my mother took me to ballet school, in through the glass door from the street, the long staircase stretched above me like a steep tunnel. The light from outside reached no farther than the bottom step, and at the top of the stairs, a single electric bulb weakly burned. The paint must have been old even then. Gray, with only the dimmest gloss, it gave off a peculiar light of its own. My legs hurt by the time we got to the landing, where a metal door with the sign, in fancy, scripted letters on an ivory background, read *Mme. S. Bartova*.

A wing of rose-colored light spread when my mother pushed the door open. On the left, daylight filtered through a set of thick, textured glass doors, framed by a much paler gray than the stairway's. On the right was an upholstered bench—also gray, but from use—and the wall, a faded sea of rose, with painted ballerinas floating on it, like mermaids or angels. Ribbon rippled from their wrists and their necks, their hair swam in waves. Their ballet costumes fitted their peach bodies like second, bright-colored skins. One costume made a blue diagonal across the top, so the dancer's right breast showed. I said, "Look." But my mother held a finger up to her lips.

There was a murmur of conversation through the glass doors. In a few minutes they opened. We saw the mother and daughter first. The girl was at least a couple of years older than I, and she didn't look happy. The mother was saying, "Thank you so much." Practically pushing them out was Madame Bartova. She was much shorter than the girl's mother, shorter than mine: a small, straight bird of a woman with a hard belly poking out from a black ballet tunic, tiny eyes in her sharp beak of a face, a bun sheathed in a hairnet on top of her head like a nest, two pink-slippered feet a broad V at the base of pink duck legs. She didn't smile. I felt myself straightening up in my shoes and squeezing tighter at my mother's hand. Bartova was a Russian name. I already knew that. She didn't speak with any strong accent, but she spoke differently from us. "So, darling. You want to send *this one* to me for ballet lessons?"

Madame Bartova sat us down on folding metal chairs. She stood facing us with the V of her feet and her open class book. Behind her was a mirror that took up one whole wall and, reflected in it, the spotless, empty studio.

"I am not a baby-sitter," she said to my mother. "My school is not a playground."

In the mirror, my mother's reflection tightened its lips. "We understand that." Madame Bartova's eyes grew even smaller as she listened. "Lisa wants very badly to study ballet. She's been begging for months now."

The lines of Madame Bartova's face softened a little, and she looked at me.

"I know the five positions," I offered. "Feet and arms too."

"And where did you learn them?"

"Lisa borrowed a book from the library," my mother said.

"I can show you." I jumped up off the chair, pulling my hand from my mother's. I started to move my saddle shoes into first position. Madame Bartova nodded grimly that I should go on. I pushed the backs of my heels together until the sides of my shoes began turning under. I cupped my hands like a basket in front of me. I lifted my chin to the ceiling. For a moment I had that feeling I'd gotten at home, practicing with the ballet book, that when I was in the position I was no longer myself. I was graceful, prettier, like the girl in the pictures.

"Stop it. This instant!" Madame Bartova shouted. "Look at those knees. And those elbows."

I tried to and lost my balance.

"Sit down, please. Now."

My mother squeezed my hand hard when I sat back down. I could see in the mirror that she was scared too.

"I'll sign Lisa up for the Tuesday beginners' class on one condition." Madame Bartova put a hand over the shiny black heart of her tunic and looked to the pair of gold toe shoes that hung on the wall, the way a religious person would look up at a cross. "She forgets every last thing she imagines she knows before she comes to me."

All the other girls' mothers picked them up after school to drive them to Madame Bartova's. My mother wasn't home from work by then, so I rode the town bus to ballet. I never saw anyone else as young as I was riding the bus alone. I sat on the front seat behind the bus driver, hugging the sticky patent leather of my ballet case close to my side, fingering the pink ballet slippers painted onto it, watching the row of shops speed into a rainbow stripe at the bottom of the bus window. The first day I had to tell the driver my stop, the Playhouse Theater, so he could make sure I got off there. After that, I'd watch for the Playhouse marquee, and kneel on the seat to reach the buzzer cord. I always pulled it a good block ahead of the stop, then stood, the strap of my ballet case on my shoulder, my toes right up to the line. I liked the way the bus doors sighed open, and the way it felt when I'd climbed down the big steps to the curb, as though I'd made a journey from one country into another.

It wasn't until I was standing in front of the Playhouse the fourth or fifth week of ballet class, the bus doors hissing shut,

that I realized I didn't have my ballet case. I raised my arm
to wave for the driver to stop, but the bus was already heaving
forward, sending off its goodbye of black smoke. In my mind
I put myself back on the bus seat. My hands had been empty
there too. I had to have left the case at the bus stop near
school. I saw the slatted wooden bench, the black patent case
forgotten there, brilliant in the fall sunlight. Maybe it would
still be there later, when my mother was driving me home.
Maybe someone would steal it. And how could I go up to
Madame Bartova's without my uniform?

While I was thinking all this, I noticed the movie poster
outside the Playhouse: a man naked except for a skin of some
kind over his crotch, his muscles shining with an oily light,
and in his raised hand, a knife glinting. My own dread got
mixed up with the dread inspired by the picture, and I must
have stared at it for some time before I pushed myself across
the street and up the block toward Madame Bartova's.

At the top of the steps, I couldn't hear anything from inside
the ballet school. I thought I must still be on time. But when
I got the door open, the scratchy music of Madame Bartova's
Victrola leaped up. Her voice cut through the notes like a
blade. One-two-three. Down-two-three. Stomachs in-two-three.
Chests out, buttocks under. Through the milky studio doors
I could see the blurred forms of black tunics like shadows, and
the larger form of Madame Bartova, her costume bleeding
deep red through the mottled smoke of the glass. Two-two-
three. Three-two-three. Just one minute.

The last words boomed through the studio and the red
shape receded, stomping its feet, sending shivers through the
wood floor, setting the glass panels vibrating. The needle
zipped off the phonograph record. Then the shape loomed up
again. It came at me from behind the glass like some great
angry bird. The doors flew open. "Lisa Reiner!" On its perch
at the top of her head, Madame Bartova's hair bun trembled.
"What are you doing standing here at this hour? Well?" Her

eyes moved from my face to my hands, suddenly heavy with their being empty. "And your uniform?"

The bus stop, I wanted to say. The bench. Madame Bartova grabbed my arm and pulled me into the light of the studio. The girls who'd been watching swung back to their spots at the barre. Each perfect black tunic arranged itself like a reproach. Even fat Chris stood there like one of the chosen.

"Do *these* girls come to class with excuses?"

I shook my bowed head.

"*My* girls come ready to work." With her pointing stick and her absolutely straight back, Madame Bartova stepped along the barre like an inspecting officer. The smug little smiles disappeared as quickly as the sun behind a dark cloud. The only sound in the studio was her slippered feet, toe-heel, toe-heel, on the floor, and beyond that, the open windows: a car horn, a sentence drifting by like a breeze. You could see the rooftops opposite through the pink organdy curtains.

"Young lady!" Madame Bartova brought her stick down hard on the floor. "Don't let me ever catch your eyes on the street once you've stepped foot inside my ballet school. You have no uniform? Speak up when you're addressing me. Chin off your chest."

My eyes traveled from Madame Bartova's turned-out feet up the tensed leg muscles. They made it as far as her mouth, the dried red color wider than her pencil lips.

"There are uniforms in the lost-and-found. But we won't interrupt the class a second time for you. There. Into the corner." She pointed to the leather hassock where she set her attendance book. "Go ahead. Sit. We don't have all day to waste."

The ballet class had never seemed so long as that day. I kept wondering what my mother would say when the doors opened after the final curtsy, the "Thank you, Madame Bartova," and I was the last to file out, in my street clothes. But

I couldn't let myself cry in the studio. It calmed me to watch the girls doing the steps, especially the older ones. A few were from the four-thirty class, and danced with us just to warm up. On their long limbs, even the simplest *relevés* and *passés* looked like something. Their shoulders were rounded soft, and their bosoms filled the tunics' curved seams. Madame Bartova never yelled at them. Now and then she'd twist a hip of one of them, take another's leg and lift it up toward the ceiling, where it would just go, as if their bodies were fastened together differently.

Would I ever be one of those girls, the ones Madame Bartova called *hers*? Just thinking of it was like looking down a road I couldn't see clear to the end of. When I'd taken out the library book on the five positions, when I'd practiced until I remembered all five, when I'd pleaded with my parents to let me go to ballet school—I'd thought I knew what it was to want something. Now my chest felt as if it couldn't contain the distance opening out in me.

I left my ballet case another time or two, lost or misplaced my tights one week, my tunic another. I could tell my right from my left standing still, but not moving; Madame Bartova made me wear an elastic hairband on my right wrist. I could do the individual steps. I practiced them diligently at home, using the edge of a Formica counter for my barre, until I'd kick or trip my mother one time too many and she'd shout, "This is a kitchen, not a ballet studio." But when Madame Bartova put together a combination, counted it once through quickly, and then said, "Right side," something got crossed between my head and my feet. The strangest movements came out sometimes.

Madame Bartova told my mother one Tuesday that it was a problem of poor attention. "She's bright enough," I heard her say while I put on my coat, as usual last in the dressing room. She said, "She's got her mind on other things," as if those other things were something in particular, something not very good.

My mother told me that night that when I was in ballet class, I had to *focus*. I had to leave everything else out on the street. I thought about what that meant, about how in my head there were songs, there was the winning play in a box-ball game during recess, there was Peter Shapiro, and Pam Schorr's nipples starting to show through her tops. I thought how it would be like the playground teacher blowing a gigantic whistle to shut all that off, to hear nothing but Madame Bartova, *one*-two-three, *one*-two-three. I got a picture of leaving all those other pieces of my day at the door to the ballet-school stairs, like dogs, to wait for me. I'd be in class trying to forget them but they'd be out there barking.

I told my mother I'd try. My father said maybe it wasn't so good to focus too much at my age, that maybe I'd be better off home with the kids on the block. My mother said, "Please. If Madame Bartova can teach her to concentrate . . ."

By fifth grade, I'd started to grow taller and skinnier. My legs still didn't fly up as high as some of the other girls'; I could spin only one pirouette; I had a problem with sticking my bottom out. But I'd gotten so I could follow combinations as well as anyone. When I was doing the steps, I thought only about my body, all the different parts of it, and in my head I heard the counting, not just Madame Bartova's but my own. It had gotten a lot easier to keep track of my costume, to comb my hair, as if I were coming out of some long fog and for the first time in my life could think clearly. Madame Bartova had begun to look at me differently, to smile ever so slightly through her thin lips, to call me "Lisie." When I did the steps across the floor and Madame Bartova didn't correct me, I could pretend I was a child ballerina, like the ones in *The Nutcracker*; that the studio floor was a stage and the tinny Victrola music an orchestra.

* * *

Madame Bartova never held a recital at the end of the year. Instead, she had what she called Open House. All the mothers and a couple of fathers came. They sat on folding chairs along the mirrored wall and watched. It was a regular lesson, except especially hard. Madame Bartova didn't hesitate to pick on you if you did badly. After the curtsy we didn't talk, but just filed out to the dressing room. Then Madame Bartova stationed herself by the door and had a word with each of the mothers.

What Madame Bartova said to my mother the first few years must not have been nice. My mother never repeated it. She just told me it had been lovely and that, yes, I'd improved. The day of fifth-grade Open House was different. When I came out of the dressing room my mother was standing with Madame Bartova. They both smiled at me. Madame Bartova put a hand on my shoulder, and the three of us stood there as if we were all in on some secret.

In the car on the way home, my mother told me: "Madame Bartova wants you to start going twice a week. The four-thirty class." She reached across the seat to straighten my collar. "She says if you work hard in the fall, then after Christmas she can start you on toe shoes."

The trees lining the main street of town were light green with new leaves, and the months of summer stretched out ahead, like a long anticipation.

For the four-thirty class, I still took the three-o'clock bus, and got to Madame Bartova's in time for the little girls' lesson. When they'd all cleared out of the dressing room and Madame Bartova had shut the glass doors, the place was mine until quarter past four or so. I was supposed to do homework, but sometimes I studied the yellowed newspaper clippings tacked to the walls, about famous ballet dancers, and listened to the muffled *one*-two-three, *one*-two-three, until I sank into a kind of trance. When the first four-thirty girl arrived, it always surprised me, as if I'd been sleeping. I'd changed into my ballet clothes when the three-thirty class started, so I sat and watched the older girls dress. That year, Madame Bartova had ordered new uniforms for the four-thirty class—wraparound costumes, pale pink. All the other four-thirty girls wore bras, even the ones with scarcely more chest than I; some fastened tiny ballet-slipper pins at the X of the wraparound bodice.

Before class, a few of the older girls sneaked out to the roof to smoke. All you had to do was climb three steps to the fire door in the dressing room. I went out there one day before anyone else came, and it wasn't much, just a square of tar paper overlooking an alleyway. I didn't care about that. What tempted me when I sat there alone was Madame Bartova's personal room, across from the bathroom. In between classes, she would sometimes disappear a minute behind the closed door, marked with a sign—"PRIVATE. KEEP OUT"—edged in the ancient, browned Scotch Tape that was on all her notices. I always pictured the room as a little apartment, with a bed, even though my mother had told me Madame Bartova lived in Queens, that she rode the Long Island Rail Road back and forth to teach each day. I could never picture Madame Bartova on the train, or walking the few blocks through town to the station. The idea of Madame Bartova in street clothes, outside the school, was like trying to imagine some exotic bird out of its natural habitat.

After the four-thirty class, if I'd been especially slow getting changed, Madame Bartova was already in her room when I was on my way out. Once she must have thought everybody had gone; she'd left her door cracked open. I was afraid to walk by, in case she should hear me, as if I'd done something wrong by still being there. The light from the room was old, golden-colored. Suddenly I had the idea that Madame Bartova was in there undressed. Only the thought of my mother waiting with her car engine on got me past the door and out

to the stairway. Night was already falling outside, headlights
and bits of neon studding the street. I wondered how long
Madame Bartova stayed in her room before she left for the
train, what kind of place she went back to.

I did get my toe shoes that Christmas, along with a half-
dozen other girls. My mother took me to the shoe store that
handled all of Madame Bartova's students. I'd never seen anything as beautiful as that sheaf of perfect pink satin, the curve
of the arch, the hard toe box. I sewed the long satin ribbons
on with demure little stitches. Somehow I figured that once
Madame Bartova said you were ready for toe shoes, you were
ready to dance in them; that you'd put them on and breeze
across the floor, your head that much closer to some upper air.
I had no idea it would be like starting over, or that it would
hurt so much.

The first time Madame Bartova had us go up on point, it
was easy. For one dizzying instant I looked over to Fran Kaplan, who was up too, and she looked back at me as if we had
both just joined the same exclusive society. But after two or
three times, gripping the barre with both hands until they
were white, pushing up and easing slowly back down—"Don't
hop down. Through your foot," Madame Bartova was shouting. "Down-two-three. Hold-two-three"—my feet started to
kill me. It wasn't so much the cramp through the arch as the
screaming across the top of my toes. I winced when Madame
Bartova wasn't looking my way. I tried to tell myself it was
just like the pain I'd already felt when Madame Bartova gave
a hard lesson.

She gave us only a few exercises on point at the barre, but
I could barely do the last ones. She clapped her hands and
said, "Toe shoes off. Back to ballet slippers," and I felt I'd
been saved. When I knelt to undo my first shoe, I knew
something was wrong. I wasn't surprised when I pulled out
my foot and saw the pink tights washed in blood. There was

also blood on the inside of the toe shoe. I hoped I could get my ballet slippers on before Madame Bartova saw. The tops of my toes stung for the rest of the class, but in a way I could bear. The worn leather ballet slippers were like gloves after the toe shoes.

Later, from the dressing-room bench, I surveyed the damage. The skin on every last toe was rubbed raw. My tights were wet and sticky with blood, though everyone else's looked perfectly clean. There must have been something peculiar about my toes; they must have been fleshier than other people's.

"God," Fran Kaplan said. "Look at that." The girls around me followed Fran's finger to my feet. "You better tell Madame Bartova."

"No, no. It's okay," I said. I put my knee socks on as quickly as I could stand to. "I just get blisters really easily."

"You better put on Band-Aids Thursday," said Daphne Berrutto, one of the older girls, "if you don't want hash for feet."

From then on, I bandaged my toes, alone in the dressing room so the other girls never saw. After class, I put my knee socks on right over my tights. Regular Band-Aids weren't enough. With my feet moving and sweating inside the toe shoes, they slipped. I got moleskin, cut one felt-soft pad for each toe and wrapped it around with adhesive tape. I perfected my system, until going on point hurt me only a little bit, the same as it must have hurt the other girls. When my mother asked about the moleskin and tape, I told her some of the other girls did it too, that being on toe was just like that. And so I learned to rise from flat feet into that precarious air, to fly in tiny steps around the room in the *bourrée*, holding my breath, thinking all the time, "Bottom under," moving my arms in waves like a bird's wings, or a real ballerina.

In seventh grade, girls started dropping out of Madame Bartova's. There were the ones who hadn't gotten picked to go on toe with me, and didn't get picked for the fall, either. A lot of the girls didn't want to go Tuesdays *and* Thursdays, even some of the ones who were good. My mother said they had other interests. Some girls changed over to the North Shore Dance Academy when it opened. North Shore didn't have only ballet; it had modern and tap and coed social dancing.

Chief among the girls' other interests was the opposite sex. Girls and boys from the junior high hung around town after school, flirting and smoking cigarettes. Some of them rode the same bus I took to Madame Bartova's; others hitchhiked or rode their bicycles. Noisy groups of kids would knot up along the sidewalks. Outside Thirty-One Flavors there were so many they were like a gang. I started to cross from the Playhouse to the other side of the street to avoid them, then cross back to slip up to Madame Bartova's.

I sat on a seat near the front of the bus, my face out the window, so the popular kids wouldn't notice me. I abandoned my ballet case for a plain canvas shoulder bag. I always had this sick feeling until I was in the dressing room at Madame Bartova's. But during the hour of ballet class, it was as if the school were ten stories up, and all the rest as distant as the street down below. I wasn't getting a chest, but my body was changing, growing longer and willowy. My face in the mirror was taking on a serious look. When we did the right side of the barre, I could watch myself. I liked the way the muscles curved hard on my calves, the way my thighs stretched unbroken into my boy hips when I copied the older girls and tucked in the tails of my wraparound. My shoulders were getting rounder with the effort of holding them down. I was hatching a secret beauty that someone would notice when it was ready.

Madame Bartova's Monday and Wednesday four-thirty class was the top of the school, the girls who were in Workshop or hoping to be in it. Workshop met for two hours on Fridays and studied parts from ballets. Rose Barton danced *The Dying Swan.* She had the longest neck I'd ever seen in my life. If she hadn't held her head up perfectly straight, it might have just toppled over. Rose went to Madame Bartova's five days a week. She had breasts like the tiniest plums, but she had a boyfriend. He waited for her outside and drove her home sometimes. Rose wanted to be a ballerina and, to listen to Madame Bartova, there was nothing stopping her. When I was in eighth grade, Rose was a senior in high school. She wasn't applying to colleges. She was going to audition in New York at company dance schools. Some of the other high school girls made fun of Rose. Instead of Rose Barton they called her Rose Bartova, because she and Madame Bartova were *like this.* When they said it, there was something dirty, the way they rubbed two fingers together.

It made me mad to hear those girls talk about Rose, but I couldn't help liking them. They had a lot more life than the Swan, who kept to herself. They'd explode into the dressing room with sodas and sandwiches from the deli next door, and give bites and sips to anybody who wanted them. They liked to read aloud from the advice columns in *Mademoiselle* and *Seventeen,* and laugh at the answers. Daphne Berrutto was the worst. High little screams would issue out of the back of her throat. Someone would have to close the dressing-room door then, even though we weren't supposed to, so Madame Bartova wouldn't hear. When Daphne had gotten over her laughing fit, Rose went to open the door, and that made Daphne start right back up again. Sometimes Rose went to sit on the hall bench to wait. Daphne would say, "I guess we're just too immature for the great Rose Bartova." Then she walked around the room like Rose, stretching her neck up as far as she could, pursing her lips, pointing her toes with each step, touching her thumbs and middle fingers together and raising her pinkies. It looked different on Daphne, with her C-cup chest and full hips, but still, it was a pretty good imitation.

The times I really didn't like Daphne were when she made fun of Madame Bartova herself, waddling around the dressing room saying, "*One*-two-three, *two*-two-three. *Screw*-two-three, *you*-two-three." It was bad enough when she did it, but what got me the most was my brother, who'd never laid eyes on Madame Bartova. He insisted on calling her Madame *Batrova*. Whenever ballet school was mentioned he stood up in an awkward V of a first position and bent his knees. "*Demi-plié. Demi-plié. Demi-plié* today." He pranced around the room, and in his most sickening girlie voice, he said, "Li-sie." The only one who called me that was Madame Bartova.

One day during class, the ribbon popped on Sheryl Turner's left toe shoe. "We wouldn't see this sort of thing," Madame Bartova said, "if you weren't neglecting the proper care of your shoes." I imagined everyone's long-suffering threads giving out all at once, a general collapse of pink satin down at our ankles. "The next time a ribbon goes in this class, there will be no point work for a month." We all had our eyes on our toe shoes, praying for strength. "We'll see how highly you value the privilege."

Madame Bartova took a deep breath. "I'll be lenient today. For the last time. Rose, would you run into the back for Sheryl? You know where I keep my safety pins."

Rose nodded and disappeared out the glass doors. There was a moment of rare suspension in the studio as we all took in the news: Rose had been inside the private room. The whole time she was gone, I listened in vain for some sound that would give away the room's secret. Her face didn't betray a thing when she came back with the safety pin.

I didn't think of the room right away, the day I realized my right inside ribbon was hanging by its last thread. I rummaged through the lost-and-found carton: gray-faded tights striped with runs, odd ballet slippers, tunics and wraparounds bearing feeble traces of bodies that had abandoned them. No safety pins. I emptied my ballet bag, held it upside down and shook. I started pacing the dressing room. The only money I had was the thirty-five cents for my bus fare—I was old enough to ride home by myself in the dark. My stomach was getting the kind of queasy feeling I'd almost forgotten from my first years at Madame Bartova's. One of the other girls might or might not have a needle and thread.

Madame Bartova was yelling at the three-thirty class. From the dressing room you could never make out exactly what she was saying. It was more like music; you picked up the mood. Each one of those girls had to be shrinking up inside herself. A bit of light from the studio opened a mouth in the shadow of the hall, and that's when I thought of it.

I stood in front of the "PRIVATE" sign for a moment, as if what I was about to enter were not just a room. The door whined on its hinges. A lamp burned in the far corner, a single bulb through a shade like ancient, yellowed parchment, that cast a strange, votive light. It was odd for Madame Bartova, who never left an extra bulb burning. The room wasn't pink and gray like the rest of the school. The walls were a rich egg cream yellow, the carpet dusty cranberry red. There was an old-fashioned cranberry divan to match, with a skin of dust and furniture oil on its clawed feet. The room had no window. On the wall where it would have been was a hulking, dark wood vanity, with a dressing glass.

Flanking the vanity was a gallery of old photographs: *corps de ballet*, rows of dancers girded stiffly with tutus, frozen in identical poses. In each picture a tiny face had been circled in pen. It was hard to be sure in that light, but the faces had an echo of Madame Bartova, what she might have looked like many years before. Then there was a double frame, a pair of ovals like breasts, with most of the gilt chipped off. The two pictures inside were big enough to see clearly. One showed a ballerina in a deep curtsy, face hidden, her head inclined in a sepia halo of gauze. The other was a simple portrait. What was surprising wasn't how different Madame Bartova looked, but how much the same. She'd been young, but she had never been beautiful. It looked as though she'd tried to gather her features into a magisterial gaze—the forbidding expression that over the years she perfected—but she hadn't altogether carried it off, and something else slipped through underneath, some disappointment or bitterness. Madame Bartova never spoke in class about her career, except to drop an occasional name— Markova, Pavlova—linked obscurely to her own past as a dancer, to what I'd always considered her fame. But I'd been mistaken. Here was the evidence. I stared again at the face in the portrait, unsure if I was sorry, or if I felt betrayed. Madame Bartova had never been more than a member of the company, nameless, practically faceless.

As I was thinking this, I heard the sound: the studio door opening, Madame Bartova's insistent toe-heel, toe-heel on the hall floor. "Hello?" She waited. "Is somebody there?" The eyes in the photograph looked back into mine for an interminable moment. At last I heard the toe-heel again, headed in the other direction. The studio door closed. I could hear the lesson start up again. I began to tiptoe out of the room, then remembered my mission.

Across the top of the vanity were smoky perfume bottles, tortoiseshell combs, a tin of dusting powder and a set of heart-shaped china boxes. I lifted each lid like the most fragile thing in the world. One box had a black hairnet, one old-fashioned plastic-quill toothpicks. And one had safety pins.

The vanity mirror was spotty and umber with age. In the parchment light, my image had the quality of the old sepia photographs. I wondered how Madame Bartova saw herself there: if she saw the woman we did or someone else—more like the young ballerina, but sharper, lovelier: somebody she might have been.

Even if you'd gone to Madame Bartova's for years, she made you come in the first week of September with your mother to register. Even then she wore a ballet costume, but she gave the impression, sitting on her hassock waiting for each girl and mother to approach her in turn, of some Old World countess receiving visitors. It was then that she made her recommendation about which classes to take, looked at you suspiciously if you had much of a suntan, reminisced with your mother about the first time she'd laid eyes on you one September afternoon, as if she hadn't ever disapproved of you, as if she'd known from the start that you'd turn into such a young lady. As the years went by, my mother came to cherish these visits. Madame Bartova would stand and take her two hands in her own, smiling like an old friend, a co-conspirator, as if together, in some unspoken pact, they had shaped me. While they talked, my mind flew about the air of the studio, executing perfect double pirouettes, a *bourrée* with steps so close there wasn't a sliver of light between two toe shoes.

In September of ninth grade, Madame Bartova talked to my mother about my coming three times a week—Monday, Wednesday, and Thursday. "Lisie should be preparing herself for the Friday Workshop. A girl cheats herself after all these years, not to take the chance to be part of a real ballet, darling. *Swan Lake. Romeo and Juliet.*" An eerie light came up in her eyes, and I thought of her small circled face in the ballet-company pictures. "*Firebird.*"

My mother took my hand, as if Madame Bartova might lead me off to a place where she could no longer reach me. "We'll have to talk to the boss."

Madame Bartova's eyes narrowed. "I hope Mr. Reiner isn't going to stand in the way of Lisie's development. After she's worked so hard."

I wasn't sure if I should be joining her in accusing my father, or defending him.

"We just have to talk it over," my mother said. "Mr. Reiner feels that Lisa should also be developing other interests."

"Other interests?" Madame Bartova leaped to her feet. "I've seen these girls ruin themselves over such stupidity. Basketball, if you can imagine. Field hockey. And when they're tired of that, you know where they go?" Her arm went out stiff in the direction of the street. "That's right, darling. You must have seen them."

My mother was almost crushing my hand by now. "Lisa was thinking about working for the student newspaper."

Madame Bartova sat back down. "Lisa has to make a choice, then." She didn't look at me when she said it. "If there's one thing my girls are not, it is dilettantes."

Dilettantes. I didn't mind the sound of the word. It seemed French, like the names of all the ballet steps. When we were on the way home, I asked.

"It's someone who does a lot of different things," my mother said.

"Isn't that good?"

"Well, what Madame Bartova means is someone who does a lot of things but never does one all the way. A dabbler."

"So if you're going to do ballet you can't be on the newspaper?"

"I guess if you were going to be a ballerina, you'd have to give up other things. But that's not what you want to be."

I was about to snap back, to say, "How do you know?" But she was right. I might still fall asleep to the vision of myself performing the slow ballet of advance and retreat with the man, like I'd seen when my mother took me to City Center. But that was already a different dream: He lifted me over his head like a breath. My legs flew up to the ceiling, not burdened with their usual gravity. There was no pain. My body wasn't this body. I thought how maybe being a dilettante wasn't so bad: to let yourself dream dishonestly; to rest in that place on the other side of the dream, on the other side of what it would take if you really wanted to get there.

The North Shore Dance Academy let boys into its ballet classes. "Of course, there are only a few," a girl who took there told me. "I don't know how they're not too embarrassed. You can see *the shape of it* right through their tights." I could never imagine that at Madame Bartova's.

Madame Bartova must not have liked men. It was easy to pretend it was all my father's fault I didn't go three times a week. He gave me permission: he said, "Make me the bad guy." So Madame Bartova didn't like me any the less. She never suspected. In fact, she started treating me with a new tenderness, as if I were a victim, as if growing up with that kind of father were like being underprivileged. She held me up as a paragon of hard work in the face of obstacles, as if, were it not for my father, my legs would go higher, the room wouldn't spin when I turned. "If Lisie can do it, the rest of you have no excuse," she'd say. She always called me Lisie now.

My mother had told her about the bandages I wore to do toe work. If she saw me limping off the floor after a combination, she knew I had a blister. Even against my protests, she made me change into ballet slippers. "Can you imagine the pain this girl puts up with?" she said to the class, as if the fact of having normal feet rendered their characters suspect. It didn't embarrass me. There was a strange kind of justice to it: making myself over in the image of my failure, I became her favorite.

Madame Bartova hadn't missed a day in thirty years of teaching. That's what she always told us. As far as she was concerned, you had to be half-dead to miss a ballet class. You had to call in advance to present your excuse. I'd turn my voice into a feeble whisper from the back of my throat, or speak through my nose, even if what I had was a stomachache.

The radiator in Madame Bartova's dressing room hissed from September to June, but there was never much heat in the studio. Still, the only time she wore her button-down sweater over her tunic was when she had a bad cold. She'd blow her nose a hundred times into the same floral-print handkerchief, folding and refolding it, and never seemed to run out of fresh places. "I'm trying to save my voice," she'd say in a stage whisper. "So give me sixty-four *échappés*." Usually, we did thirty-two. I was never sure what one thing had to do with the other.

There was absolutely no precedent for the day I got to Madame Bartova's and found the door locked. The hallway was dark and there was no sound of movement inside. I heaved my shoulder into the door's metal. The noise I made didn't echo but left a hollow vibration. It was hard to think. Why weren't any of the other girls there? Was it some holiday I'd forgotten? Had Madame Bartova made an announcement I'd missed? I listened at the door again. I sat on the top step and waited. Nobody came. I took the four-o'clock bus home. The sounds of the street came to me as if from across a great distance.

My mother was at the kitchen table when I got home, her hands folded in front of her. She just looked at me.

"Don't you want to know what I'm doing home?" My ballet bag sank, forlorn, onto the table.

"I know," she said. She patted the seat of the chair next to hers.

"You do?"

What surprised me most wasn't the news that Madame Bartova was "no longer with us." It was the fact that the calls to all the girls' homes had been made by her sister. She'd never mentioned a sister; never said a word about a life outside her girls.

The way I visualized Madame Bartova's death was as the white spaces on a calendar, blank slots of time where her classes had been. On the ballet-company pictures she'd hung in her room, I imagined holes in place of her circled faces. Though I'd never seen the sister, I couldn't help hating her for stealing Madame Bartova's death from us. She had all of our numbers. She could have invited the older girls, the girls who'd been with Madame Bartova for years, to the funeral. I pictured Madame Bartova in her coffin, dressed in a new, pink-pink pair of tights, her best tunic, the gold toe shoes that had hung all those years on the wall. The music for *Swan Lake*, only not scratchy, would play in the background. The girls would walk up with a flourish, toe-heel, toe-heel, shoulders back and chins up, so anybody could see we were proud. I was sure that's the way Madame Bartova would have wanted it.

I didn't switch to the North Shore Dance Academy like most of the girls. Madame Bartova had always looked on the girls who left her school for North Shore as traitors. I decided to just keep practicing on my own, with Madame Bartova's *one*-two-three, *one*-two-three inside my head. A couple of times a week, I wrapped my toes in their full moleskin and adhesive-tape regalia. I pinned up my hair. I kept my uniform as scrupulously clean as I had for ballet class. Holding on to the edge of the kitchen sink, I went through the whole barre, and a point barre. I did the *bourrée* across the stone floor of the den. There was only one part I did differently. When my toes started to smart, I put my ballet slippers back on and got out an album, Cat Stevens or Jackson Browne. There were certain sad, slow love songs that were great for ballet. Even Madame Bartova couldn't have hated them.

While the needle ran the silence before a song, I set myself up: kneeling on one knee, my face pressed into it, my arms crossed in an attitude like prayer in front of me. I was still for the first plaintive notes, then I slowly opened my body. I didn't think of doing one step or another. The steps just came to my body like breath, flowed one into the next as if they issued out of the music. There was no one to correct me, no mirror. It seemed to me that my dancing was as beautiful and as sad as the song. Sometimes I imagined an audience, sometimes that I was dancing on the stage of an empty auditorium. Someone had tiptoed in but I hadn't noticed him. To the final chords of piano or guitar, I made my body into a cave again. I held my fast breath a few seconds, then stood. That would be when I saw him. I was never good at imagining the ordinary things that would happen after that moment, the things we might say. If he opened his mouth to speak, he might have braces, he might utter something ridiculous.

Over the months, my practicing did become less and less frequent. Sometimes I skipped the barre and the toe shoes altogether, and just put on a record to dance. With all my afternoons free, I started working a lot for the newspaper. Junior year, I was voted Arts Editor, and took the Creative Writing class. I began to think about how minds were better than bodies. There was nothing like gravity working against them. They weren't so fast to forget. I could still see Madame Bartova perfectly; her voice came to me at odd times of the day, in its own exact timbre. Yet in the year since she'd died, my dances had settled into variations on the same half-dozen steps. There were so many more, I knew. But my feet had trouble remembering.

About the Author

Ellen Lesser, A Yale graduate, teaches in the Master of Fine Arts in Writing Program at Vermont College. Her short stories, book reviews, essays, and interviews have appeared in *The Village Voice, Mississippi Review, Epoch, New England Review/Bread Loaf Quarterly,* and other magazines.

She grew up on Long Island and now lives in Vermont.